PUFFIN BOOKS

Faerie Heart

Livi Michael is the author of four novels for adults and the bestselling series of books about Frank the hamster for younger children. She has two sons and lives in Manchester.

D1142801

LIVI MICHAEL

Faerie Heart

PUFFIN

PUFFIN BOOKS

Published by the Penguin Group
Penguin Books Ltd, 80 Strand, London WC2R ORL, England
Penguin Group (USA) Inc., 375 Hudson Street, New York, New York 10014, USA
Penguin Group (Canada), 90 Eglinton Avenue East, Suite 700, Toronto, Ontario, Canada M4P 2Y3
(a division of Pearson Penguin Canada Inc.)
Penguin Ireland, 25 St Stephen's Green, Dublin 2, Ireland (a division of Penguin Books Ltd)
Penguin Group (Australia), 250 Camberwell Road, Camberwell, Victoria 3124, Australia
(a division of Pearson Australia Group Pty Ltd)
Penguin Books India Pvt Ltd, 11 Community Centre, Panchsheel Park, New Delhi – 110 017, India
Penguin Group (NZ), 67 Apollo Drive, Rosedale, North Shore 0632, New Zealand
(a division of Pearson New Zealand Ltd)
Penguin Books (South Africa) (Pty) Ltd, 24 Sturdee Avenue, Rosebank, Johannesburg 2196, South Africa

Penguin Books Ltd, Registered Offices: 80 Strand, London WC2R ORL, England

puffinbooks.com

First published 2009
1

Text copyright © Livi Michael, 2009
All rights reserved

The moral right of the author has been asserted

Set in 11.5/15pt by Palimpsest Book Production Limited, Grangemouth, Stirlingshire
Made and printed in England by Clays Ltd, St Ives plc

British Library Cataloguing in Publication Data
A CIP catalogue record for this book is available from the British Library

ISBN: 978-0-141-31925-4

www.greenpenguin.co.uk

Penguin Books is committed to a sustainable future
for our business, our readers and our planet.
The book in your hands is made from paper
certified by the Forest Stewardship Council.

To my niece Freya,
who looks a little like the Keri in this book

PART I

A long time ago, when the earth was white and the seas were frozen, Guri stole fire from the faeries . . .

That's how the story goes. I know it off by heart – we all do. But I'm waiting by the fire for everyone to arrive, so that we can hear it all over again.

Rain's blowing hard against our hut as we let people in. Some of it's blowing in through the hole in the roof and the fire's gone out twice. Still, it's the first moon of autumn, and we're gathering here like always to hear Myrna tell our tale.

Bryn's fussing around as usual, getting everyone seated by the fire. Myrna has to be helped down on to our stool by Mabda, her daughter. You can almost hear her bones creak as she settles in. The rest of us sit on the floor, trying not to notice how damp it is. Everyone's coughing because of the smoke. I hitch my little brother, Lu, further up my knee and try to stop him pulling my hair. Digri pulls a face at me and grins. My mother pokes the fire again, and passes the pot around so that we can have a drink, then we all turn our damp, grimy faces towards Myrna, and she looks back at us keenly, though her eyes are near enough blind.

She takes a long swig from the pot, and hands it back to my mother. Then she begins, in her rasping voice.

'In the First Days,' she says, 'the land was filled with magic. There were spirits in the trees and the hedgerows, in pools of water and mossy caves. When the People came, digging the land, and chopping down trees and changing the way of rivers and streams, they fled to underground caverns, and chambers beneath the sea, or to the dark heart of the forest. Some of them left entirely, travelling on the Lost Paths to unknown lands, but those who stayed tried to defeat us by magic, causing rivers to flood and forests to burn, setting loose our animals at night, and turning fields of barley to rubble and stones. They are worse enemies than the wind and rain, because they mean us harm, and more deadly than the raiders, because only if they allow it can they be seen.'

I've tried to see one. Sometimes I think I have – or nearly. When I've gone further into the forest than I should, picking sticks. Where the light changes and one thing starts to look like another. You can hear them sometimes – little scuttering noises in the hedgerows, tiny footsteps pattering like rain on the leaves. If you see one before it sees you it can be made to talk, and you can ask it questions. But if they show themselves to you, it's almost always trouble. They can take any shape they like, tall as a tree, fiery and beautiful, or soft, like mist on the river. They are the *Sith*, or faerie folk, and mostly we try to drive them out. But I would like, just once, to see a faerie.

'The strongest and fiercest of all the faerie folk is Mabb. She haunts the forest and the hillsides, looking for the rest of her folk who have been driven away, or trying to lure the People into her faerie world, or trick us into doing her will. They say that for every faerie she's lost she will take one of the People. And those who are lured into her realm rarely find their way out again.'

I bet I would, though. If I met Mabb, I wouldn't be afraid of her. I'd ask her what she did all day, and get her to show me her magic. We'd fly through the air like birds, or float underwater. We'd hide in flower cups or the roots of trees. We'd spin webs with the spiders and make honey with the bees. It's not true that you can't find your way back from the faerie world – Guri did. Myrna's telling his story now.

'Long ago, when the hard winters came, and the earth was white and even the seas were frozen, Guri followed a dancing light over a frozen moor,' she says. 'The flame changed colour and was sometimes blue, sometimes red and sometimes a cold, fierce yellow.

'The wind battered Guri, and snow and ice froze his bones. At last he came to a lonely spot on a hill, where mist curled from the earth in a circle. "I will die here," he thought, and he lay down. But some time later he woke up, bathed in a golden light. Outside the circle snow fell and the wind howled, but inside was warm and bright, and there was a table, set with food. At one end of it sat a woman such as he had never seen. Fiery hair fell below her knees, and round her head there was a little circlet of flames. Guri thought that he must have died after all, but he was warm, warmer than he had ever been, and he had thought he would never be warm again. The woman smiled at him and said, "Welcome," and her voice was like the crackling of fire over leaves.

"'Eat," she said, "and drink."

'Now Guri was hollow with hunger, for all his People had been starving through the long winter. But Guri knew that he mustn't eat or drink with the faeries, or he might never leave their world, and he was feared, for the woman was wild and strange as the moor itself. So he rose and sat at the table, but he didn't touch a thing.

"'Are you not hungry?" she asked him, but Guri could only stare at her fiery hair which lit up the scene around him. Sparks fell from it on to the table like candles, lighting up all the food. He thought it was the most beautiful thing he had ever seen.

"'Who are you?" he asked.

"'My name is Mabb, Queen of the Faeries," she said, pouring a golden drink into a bowl. "Why don't you eat?"

'Guri could only shake his head. He found it hard to speak, for the drink smelled of summer, and the perfume of it filled his mind.

'"What do you want?" she asked him.

'"I have come for my People," he said. "They cannot survive another winter without fire to keep them warm."

'"There is no hurry," said the Lady. "These flames will never die. Stay and eat with me."

'"If I do," said Guri, "will you give me the secret of fire?"

'Mabb's voice rustled like laughter. "What will you give me?" she asked.

'"What can I give you?" asked Guri.

'Mabb looked at him with her mocking eyes. "A kiss," she said.

'But Guri knew that if he kissed her, he might never leave. "I may not kiss you, Lady," he said, and Mabb's smile became more mocking still.

"You have followed me so far," she said. "Will you go home empty-handed? A simple kiss is all I ask."

'Then Guri spoke these words to her:

> *The wolf has his pelt,*
> *And the raven his wing,*
> *But I have my immortal soul.*

'Mabb shrugged. "One spark for another," she said, and all around him the scene began to crumple and shrivel, as if it was burning up before his eyes.

'Then Guri stood up quickly. "Wait!" he cried, and with one hand on his knife, he approached her.

'Though Guri was tall, the Lady had to stoop to kiss him. But before he could feel her lips on his, he reached up and cut off a strand of her burning hair, then stepped back quickly.

'Mabb was so angry that sparks flew from her hair and eyes. "You take that which is not given," she said. "You must leave something in exchange."

'Guri held the burning strand in his left hand, and his shadow fell to the right. But now Mabb lifted her hand and his shadow left him, and went to stand at her side. A shiver passed through Guri. But he held up the lock of her hair like a torch and stepped out of the circle of light, into the whirling storm.

'The wind blew and the snow and hail fell, but the burning strand didn't go out. It burned Guri as he held it, and the left side of his body was scorched by the fire. Yet he struggled on, until he came to the huts of his People.

'"I have brought you this Gift," he said, and he sat down, shaking like a leaf in winter. His left side had withered like bark on a tree, or a twisted branch, struck by lightning. But he had brought to his People the Gift of fire, for the flaming strand never did go out.

And the People warmed themselves by it, and lit more fires throughout the long harsh winters that covered the earth in those days almost all the year round. And they learned to cook and make weapons and tools, so that they survived and grew strong, and spread from one shore to another, until the earth itself grew warm again.

'But it was said of Guri that he never grew older, and that even on the brightest day he cast no shadow. With his left eye he could see only visions of the faerie world, with his left hand he could feel Mabb's fingers and with his left foot he could find the faerie pathways. And at long last, when everyone he loved on this earth had died, he returned to the shadow he had left at Mabb's side. But we, the People, grew strong, because of the Gift of fire.'

Tricksy folk, faeries, everyone knows that. Set babies crying all night. Turn milk sour in the cow, and set hens to laying pebbles instead of eggs. You never really get the better of them. But sometimes I wonder if you could try being friends with them. I don't think anyone's ever tried.

You can still see the hill where Guri met Mabb. It's all speckled with stones, which are all the People who've ever looked for Mabb, or crossed her in some way, and it has a cleft in the top like a dimpled chin. Mabb's Hill, we call it, but we aren't allowed to go up there. If you light a fire on Mabb's Hill, at the right time, Myrna says, she'll come for you.

'What is the right time?' I asked her, but she only gave me one of her looks.

'You'll be sorry if she comes for you,' she said.

Myrna's still speaking, but now her story's taken a sad turn. Because the People aren't strong any more. After years of bad winters, bad summers, bad harvests, the creeping sickness, the shaking sickness, and the raiders, all that's left of us is five small huts huddled between the forest and Mabb's Hill.

'These are the five households of the People,' Myrna says, and she names us all.

There's mine, of course, with my mother and Bryn, my father's brother, and Lu, who was named for my father.

Myrna and Mabda, her daughter, and Arun, Mabda's grandson, who lives with them since his father was killed with mine. But Arun's not here now, because he was sick this morning and has to stay in his bed.

My friend Digri, with Griff, his father, and little Ogda.

Gwern, Griff's brother, with Orla and Peglan and Derry.

Arval, with Tilse, in the hut where Arun used to live.

Long ago, the land we live in was part of a much bigger land. The People came to it on foot, following the herds of deer and wild horses. We had no huts, no crops; we just followed the animals and hunted them. Then the big winters came and when the ice cracked, the land cracked with it, leaving us on an island. The People didn't mind. We didn't have to follow the animals so far, and soon we learned how to keep them in one place so that we could build our huts and grow our own food.

But not everyone was happy. There were other folk here when we first came. Wild men of the woods who lived like animals and fled when they saw us. Some of them turned raiders, attacking our huts, and taking our food.

They're still there, giving us trouble. My father died when the raiders came. Tall savage men, wearing nothing but paint on their bodies. Howling like wolves and not seeming to feel the cold. Women and children had to crouch in the underground hide, while my father and his brothers, Bryn and Arval, together with Griff, his brother Gwern and Magda's two sons, all fought the raiders with arrows and spears. Digri says he fought too, but he never did. He stayed in the hide with me, crying like a girl.

My father was pierced by a spear, and all Myrna's healing arts could not bring him back from the Land of Shadows. And Mabda lost both her sons that day, and was sick with grieving. And my mother, who was already carrying my brother, looked likely to die herself. But Myrna nursed her with wild primrose and nettles, and raspberry leaves, and before the year was out my brother was born, and named Lu, which was our father's name.

I shift and sigh and try to get comfortable. Lu whines when I move him and Myrna looks sharply my way, eyes like curdled milk. But I know this part of the story by heart anyway. We all do. It doesn't make us feel good to hear it. Because it's not a good story, and no one knows how it'll go on.

'There may not be many of us left,' Myrna says, 'but there is new life.' She glances round at the youngest ones, at Lu and Ogda, Peglan and Derry, and the baby that is in Tilse's stomach. 'And where there is new life, there is always hope. May the land keep you, and may the People keep the land.'

She finishes, making the sign of protection against the *Sith*, and she looks round at us all just as if she could see us, as if she's waiting for an answer, or another end to her tale.

In the silence that follows I look at my mother, but her head's bowed so low that her plaits are sweeping the floor. Then I look at Digri, but he's picking at the floor with his new knife. Little Ogda's sitting next to him, her two short braids sticking straight out from her head, two candles of snot from her nose. Peglan and Derry are sleeping already, on their mother's knee. Everyone else is watching the shapes in the fire, and I can see, plain as day, what they're thinking. They're remembering, though none of us was alive then, not even Myrna, the days when the People were strong and great. But now there are only five households left, and another hard winter coming. Beavers build their dams high and the wolves' pelts grow thick. That's what they're thinking.

I hitch my little brother further up my knee. His head's heavy on my arm, and my leg's gone dead. Plus he's started to drool, and there's a big wet patch near my shoulder. Disgusting. Then Griff, Digri's father, stirs at last.

'We need another Gift,' he says.

No one says anything to this. My mother gets up and starts raking the fire, then, with much huffing and sighing, everyone starts to leave. Mabda helps Myrna to her feet; Digri carries Ogda. My mother sweeps the ashes from round the fire.

'Put Lu to bed, Keri,' she says, and she stands the broom against the wall. Bryn comes back from checking that the pigs are safely penned in. 'Sleep well, Keri,' he says.

I barely nod at him as I carry Lu through the sackcloth hanging that divides our room from the main one, then put him down on my bed.

He wakes up, of course, and whimpers till I lie down with him myself. Then he turns his warm wet bum into my stomach and sucks his fingers. The sackcloth's bumpy over the rushes and I kick at it to bed it down. And kick again when I feel something running lightly over my foot. A mouse. I can hear my mother and Bryn talking in the next room – Bryn saying how he might keep watch in case the animals come untethered again tonight, and my mother saying that the faerie folk don't like being spied on. Then they start putting out the charms to keep the faeries away – hanging a rowan branch over the door and nailing a piece of dried bread beneath it. Digri made a charm of bird bones and feathers for the front of his hut. Only Myrna leaves food out for them, barley and apples and nuts.

'Why do you?' I asked her.

'Respect,' she said. She wouldn't say any more. But I wondered if that was how she learned to do her magic – if she made friends with them before she came to us.

I would like to make friends with them.

I close my eyes and see long, witchety fingers picking at the gate. My own fingers find the amulet that's round my neck. The one my father made. I could go out and keep watch, but they'd never let me. Yet no matter how Bryn ties the gates, they're always undone and the pigs and chickens running wild, come morning.

Bryn's all right, but he has no luck. He's not my father. We were getting by, my mother and me, after Lu was born. I helped her look after the baby and did all the chores as well. Then in the spring Bryn staked his claim. He was single and my mother free. Every household should have a man, he said. My mother held out against him at first, but at harvest time he moved into my father's hut.

'Every household doesn't need a man,' I told my mother. 'Myrna and Mabda live together, alone.'

'But they are old,' my mother said. 'Anyway,' she added, 'we need someone to look after us.'

'I'll look after us!' I said, and my mother sighed and shook her head.

'We need more children,' she said, and I didn't say anything to that. That was too much to think about.

Now they're arguing in hushed tones as if they think I can't hear.

'– time she stopped playing,' I hear Bryn say. 'We must give her more work.'

I listen hard, but my mother says nothing to this. I can hear her turning away from him. Bryn will never take the place of my father, not even in my mother's heart. And he knows that.

Lu elbows me in the ribs and I shove him so that he lies further away. He could sleep in his own cradle if he wanted to, but he always wants to sleep with me. And keep me awake.

They are arguing again, about the roof that needs thatching. My mother says that Bryn's leaving it too long, and Bryn says that the dyke comes first.

My father would have thatched the roof.

If I could do magic I'd mend the roof.

I'd bring my father back.

The night has grown quiet now, a special kind of quiet, full of the noises you forget to hear in the daytime. Apart from my mother and Bryn. The sound of their muttering mingles with the murmuring of the forest, and Lu's breathing, and I turn over, curling into him, and clutch the amulet my father made. And nothing changes, I can't make it change, but I do start to feel just a tiny bit better.

I shift again on the bumpy sackcloth, and scratch myself, and try to sleep. I can hear the forest talking now. Behind everything there is always the sound of the forest. Boughs creaking, branches moaning, and water running in little rivulets and talking to itself. The great dark trees of the forest stand all around our little huts. Beyond them are trees, and beyond them, more trees. As far as anyone can go to the north, east and west, for a day, a week, or a whole month, there are only trees. All pathways end just a little way in. Then there are no huts and no People, but only the wild animals – wolves and bears and deer, foxes and badgers and birds. The forest is a whole world. It feeds us and gives us wood for shelter and warmth, but it is as dangerous as a wild beast, Myrna says. No one goes into it and leaves again unchanged.

She says that the spirits of the People live in the trees and whisper together at night. Somewhere in there my father crouches in the bole of a tree, or is stretched out in its branches, watching us. And his parents, and their parents, and Digri's mother, and Mabda's two sons. When the wind moans in the branches she says they are mourning their mortal lives. The trees watch over us as we go in, and that's why we must pick wood only from the forest floor, and never, ever, hurt a tree.

My mother and Bryn stop arguing, finally, and now I can only hear the voices of the forest. 'Who – who?' cries an owl, and the night hawk cries 'Here – over here'. If I listen closely I can hear all the night creatures settling in branches or scurrying through roots. Closer still, and the forest seems to be calling my name.

'Keri,' it whispers. 'Ke-ri.'

Next day there's work to do before I can go out and play. Sweeping the hut, minding Lu, who tips over his bowl of porridge then crawls around in it, so that I have to clean him up. Then I have to feed the hens and the pigs. I take Lu with me, though it's hard to hang on to him and feed the pigs at the same time.

I can hear the shouts of the men by the river. They are rolling clods of earth and large stones to make a dyke to stop the fields flooding when the rains come. First they fell trees with their stone axes that are always breaking. They're allowed, because we all need the wood from the trees, and because they make offerings first, to the forest. They hack the branches off the trunks until they're left with smooth logs. They roll the biggest stones along on these logs, but it's hard, heavy work. The ground's uneven and the stones fall off. Someone must always keep moving the logs from the back to the front, and they slither and slide in the mud.

If we were friends with the faeries, we wouldn't have to work so hard. They'd teach us their magic.

Digri and the others are gathering clay from the riverbed to make into pots, but I have to stay here with Lu, while my mother picks the last of the crops. She comes back through the field with a basket of peas and beans.

'If you get all these shelled for the stew,' she says, 'you can go and play with the others.'

I'm sick of shelling peas and weaving baskets just because I'm a girl. But at least my mother's taken Lu now, so I don't have to look after him. I sit down with a sigh in the doorway of our hut, and start splitting the pods.

Tilse comes over to join me with her own basket.

Not long ago I would have played with Tilse, but now she is married to Arval, my father's youngest brother. Tilse is Mabda's youngest, hardly older than me. Before the raiders came, she ran in the forest and paddled in the river with the rest of us, but now she works with the women and waits for her baby in the spring. That's all she talks about now. It's all anyone talks about – new life for the People.

'I was sick again this morning,' she says to me.

Don't want to know.

'But I don't mind so much now,' she says. 'It means the baby's thriving, Myrna says, the sicker you are. But I was up three times in the night, passing water.'

I bend over my bowl, shelling the peas as fast as I can.

'You don't keep the brown ones,' she tells me. 'Just the little, sweet green ones. When I got back to bed the third time, I couldn't sleep. Then I thought I felt him kicking! Though it's very early, Myrna says.'

I look at her. 'You don't know it's a boy,' I say, and she smiles smugly.

'Mothers know. Myrna says that she knew, every time. When you're a mother, you'll know.'

'I don't want to be a mother,' I tell her, but she only laughs at me and tells me I'll change my mind.

I stare at her. Her nut-brown hair is lank and dull; her cheeks, that used to be round and pink, are pale. 'Maybe I won't,' I say.

'Well, you'll have to one day,'

'I don't have to!'

'Everyone has to, sooner or later. Or how will the People survive?'

I don't know how the People will survive. But I don't want to spend my whole life having babies.

I don't want to grow up.

I don't want to marry.

And I definitely don't want to breed, like a sow.

'There's nothing special about having babies,' I tell her. 'Even the pigs do it.' But she only smiles at me in that grown-up way that means she thinks she knows so much better than me.

'I'm going to play with Digri.' I tell her. 'You could come with us if you like. Oh – no, you can't – you've got to stay in your hut and cook for your husband.'

I can't see her face, bent low over the peas in her basket, but she says, very slyly, 'Maybe one day you will live in Digri's hut.'

Something about the way she says this makes me feel it's already been discussed, and I'm so angry that I knock over the bowl of peas she's shelling and run off.

It's not hard to follow the sound of the others, shouting and laughing by the river. Before I get there Digri comes to meet me by the water-lily pond. He is red-faced and cheerful as usual, whistling and whittling a stick. Digri is my best friend, but I wouldn't want to live with him in his hut. His mother died having Ogda, and his father is a red-faced, angry man, mean as his dogs. I'm glad my mother didn't marry him, and I definitely wouldn't want to marry Digri.

'I was just coming for you.' he says. 'We're building a dam by the river,'

I look at the flat leaves floating on the surface of the still pond. I'm hungry, and the bulbs are good to eat. I wade into the pond. The water is freezing cold and the flowers have all gone, but I pluck two bulbs and hold one out to Digri. 'Let's play Mabb and Guri,' I say.

Digri takes a bite out of the bulb and I say, 'Ha! Mortal – you have eaten my faerie food! Now you must do as I ask!'

Digri pulls a face at this because he knows the game. He has to do three things I tell him to and try to catch me out. Then he can stop being my slave. So when I tell him he has to catch a fish with his bare hands, he dives under the water, then grabs my knees and I go under with him, coughing and spluttering. He won't let me go until I release him from my spell. I shout and kick and splutter, but he just hangs on.

'All right, all right!' I yell. 'You can be Mabb now, and I'll be Guri.'

But Digri doesn't want to be Mabb.

'You're the girl,' he says. But I'm always Mabb, and sometimes I want to be Guri. Guri was a hero.

'A girl can't be Guri,' Digri says. 'Girls can't be warriors.'

'I can be,' I tell him, but he shakes his head, stubborn as a tree-stump. 'I'm going to build that dam,' he says.

I might be a girl, but I'm older than he is, and he used to do everything I told him. Now he only wants to play with Arun.

'We can go up Mabb's Hill,' I tell him. 'And you can push me off.'

I like rolling down Mabb's Hill. But last time, when I pushed Digri off, he hurt his ankle. He shakes his head.

'We're not allowed,' he says.

'*Please*,' I beg, but I know that look on his face.

'I'm going to build a dam, and spear fish,' he says, turning away.

I throw a handful of small stones after him, but he doesn't even look round. That's how it always is these days. Digri plays with Arun, Little Ogda and Peglan trail behind. Lu and Derry are too young yet for playing. They stay with the women, in the huts. So that leaves no one for me.

I can play by myself, or go back and help my mother with the housework, or tag along behind Digri and Arun. It's not fair. I wish I had someone else to play with.

I wade out a little further into the pond, and twist a root out. I can see cloud shadows in the water, and my own head, staring down. Then I can see Mabb's Hill.

I look at the reflection of it in the water. They say you can get into the faerie world through the reflections in water. I would like, more than anything, to travel there, on the glimmering roads, where every wish becomes real. I imagine slipping through the water into a different world. What would it be like, in that world? Everything would be upside down, the rain falling upwards, and little streams running uphill, and I would run with them, easy and quick. I could make myself small, like the kernel of a nut, or fly about in the wind like thistlefluff. I wouldn't have to go back to my ordinary world and do boring jobs because I'm a girl, or turn into a woman and have babies.

I look up at the real hill. I'm not allowed to travel up there alone, or to light a fire. Anyway, I don't know how. Bryn showed me once, and I tried, rubbing the point of one stick into a notch cut in another, but it took ages, and no smoke appeared, and I just got cross. Bryn laughed and said that the sticks were probably green inside.

It would be easier to slip into the water, and up that hill.

I bend down low over it and whisper, 'Mabb – can you hear me?'

Nothing happens, except that my breath makes ripples on the water. Then I pick one of the hollow reeds and blow through it.

'Come out, Mabb,' I call, blowing bubbles into the water. 'Come out, wherever you are . . .'

A surprised frog plops into the water from a water-lily leaf, but nothing else happens. I watch little minnows swimming together beneath the surface. The minnows are like thin grey shadows in the water, and now and then one of them flashes sunshine from its silvery belly. The air smells of damp roots and mud. I straighten up, putting water-lily leaves on my head, and in my reflection they look like a crown. Don't know why I say it, it just comes into my mind and out of my mouth.

'Who is queen now?' I ask.

Then I see them, hovering over the water, a little swarm of white moths. They are facing me, and perfectly still, except for the whirring of their wings. I look at them, and I know they are looking at me. I have never seen anything like them before. It's not the right time for moths. Suddenly afraid, I turn and splash out of the pond, hurrying to join the others by the river.

Feels like walking through a dream. Already I'm not sure I saw anything at all. Without thinking, I follow the sound of voices towards the river, and when Digri leaps out at me I stare at him as though I've never seen him before. He's splashed with mud and there are bits of weed and leaves clinging to him.

'We're making a dam,' he says. 'Come on!'

I look at the river. We're not supposed to go in the broad part, where the men are building the dyke. But this part of it's only a stream, branching off from the main bit, babbling peacefully along. Even Ogda's in there, up to her knees in the shallow water, her tunic floating around her. Cautiously, I step into the chilly water.

The gravel hurts and mud swirls where I put my feet. Midges swarm around my face. When I lift a rock, more mud swirls like sandy smoke and tiny creatures flee for cover. Peglan sits down *plop* in the water and Ogda follows, their backsides black and wet. They've all forgotten about digging out clay for pots. Together we build our dam, hoping to trap fish.

Slowly, the light shifts. The willows rustle and breathe and the water talks to itself in the dusk. We work on in silence, concentrating on getting the rocks in place. I remember the moths hovering, facing towards me. I should have gone right up to them, and let them land all over me with their fluttering wings. They might have lifted me up, and taken me into the faerie world. But I didn't let them. I ran away.

The back of my neck starts to hurt from bending low over the water. Building the dam is slow, and dull. I want something else to happen. Something magical. I wade further upstream, towards a bend in the river, waving at Digri to follow. When we get to the bend I grab his arm.

'Look,' I say.

Further on, near the curve where the stream joins the river, something is moving by the riverbed. A grey shape in the grey dusk, leaning forwards. It could be an otter or a beaver, but as it dips towards the water, suddenly I know what it is. The Peggotty Witch.

The Peggotty Witch is one of the faerie folk – a little washerwoman. She washes bloodstained clothing in deserted streams, and if it's your clothing, you are bound to die. Tilse said she saw her before the raiders came, washing a great pile of bloodstained clothes. I look at Digri, and at Arun who has splashed up behind him, and they look at me. Peglan and Ogda are poking under stones with a stick, and don't even look up.

'It's the Peggotty Witch,' I tell them.

They look at me as if they don't know whether to believe me or not, so without saying a word I start to creep along the bank, picking up a stone, and Digri and Arun follow me with sticks.

Don't know what we'll do when we get to her. She's terribly ugly, they say, with green skin and webbed feet, and one huge nostril, like a hole in her face, and one long jaggly tooth in her mouth. She doesn't talk properly, but mumbles and grunts. If you see her before she sees you, and catch hold of her washing, you can ask her three questions and she must answer you true. But if she strikes at your legs with the wet washing you will lose all power in them, and float away in the water like so much washing. Besides, she brings death with her, like I said, so it's best always to drive her away with sticks and stones.

Closer and closer we creep, until we can hear a thin tuneless drone, like humming. It makes my blood freeze and my heart pump in my ears. Maybe it is the Peggotty Witch; maybe she really is there. And now I'm sure I can see the shadow of her in the twilight, all wrapped up in grey cloth like a shroud.

The bank gets steeper and we climb along it until we're almost directly above the grey shape, and no one has made a sound or even cracked a twig. Then Arun's foot slips and a shower of small stones scatter down.

Quick as a ferret the grey shrouded shape whips into the water. 'NOW!' I shout, and we skid down the bank yelling and waving our sticks. I look for green skin and a face with a hole in it, but there's nothing there. I leap off the bank and land, crouching at the water's edge, and grab another stone. Digri's stick whistles through the air and Arun's stone lands in the water, and we all stumble and run downstream, splashing after her as far as we dare, but the water's getting deep, and all we can see is a dark shape scuttling through it, fast as a moorhen after its chicks. It's hard to believe how fast she can go. She rounds the bend and disappears up the bank, a grey shape in the grey dusk, and we stand together chanting:

> *Peg leg, pig leg,*
> *Pick up your rags and beg,*
> *Never come here more!*

We daren't follow her further, leaving Peglan and Ogda behind, but as she disappears we turn to one another and raise our fists and whoop our victory, until we're hoarse. Then I notice how dark it's getting.

'It's late,' I say. 'We've got to get back.' And I turn and run ahead of them, back to where Peglan and Ogda are waiting. They've noticed we've gone and set up loud complaints as we return, but Digri picks up Ogda and Arun pulls Peglan along, and wet and muddy we make it back to our huts for the evening meal.

Though there are only five households, we all take a lot of feeding. Everyone works all day long to prepare for the winter. The next day Griff and Gwern decide to kill one of their pigs. Bryn and Arval make a fire and heat water over it. Griff brings his long knife. Me and Digri, Arun and Peglan and Ogda run and hide in the long ditch, and stuff our fingers in our ears so that we can't hear the pig squealing. I hate to see the pigs being butchered because I feed them every day. They nudge and jostle and grunt as though they are pleased to see me. Friendlier than the dogs, that are only for hunting.

When the pig stops squealing, we look out cautiously. Griff and Gwern are scraping its bristles off with a knife. They will take out the insides and hang it in a tree. My mother catches sight of us watching.

'Take the others to play, Keri,' she says. 'But come back before it gets dark.' We wander off slowly, kicking stones. Once the hog is butchered there will be good meat right through the winter. Every part of it will be used, the heart and liver and tongue, and Bryn will blow up the bladder for us to play with. Still, none of us likes losing a pig.

Arun wants to play by the river again, but I want to go into the forest.

'We're not allowed to go into the forest,' Arun says, but I say that no one is watching. 'Anyway, it's my turn,' I tell him.

I lead the way, going from one tree to another, further and further in. The paths are made by animals, not People, and they soon disappear, then another one starts. We're not supposed to follow the tracks because they don't lead anywhere, but it's easy to forget that. It's easy to forget everything in the forest.

Just in time, Digri says, 'I'll make a mark on the trees,' and he scrapes at one with his new knife.

We've all been taught how to leave a trail, though we're not supposed to cut the trees. Digri only scratches them so that it doesn't hurt. And it's better than getting lost. Already the light has changed and the air too. You can almost hear the forest breathing.

Things I can't see scuttle away from my feet. The floor of the forest is all tangled ivy and roots, great twisted roots that will seize you and drag you into the earth. I've never been so far in before. We're allowed to pick sticks just from the edges, and sometimes we dare one another to go further in, but never this far. This is where the faeries live. And the raiders.

I know I should turn back. I should take the others home now, before all the light fades. If anyone finds out we'll be in trouble, especially me, because I'm the oldest. But Digri's still making his marks, and besides, I feel as though something's calling me, further on and deeper in. Then I stumble over a long root, and when I look up I see it, a great, thick tree, about a thousand years thick, with a big hollow space in its trunk. As soon as I see it, I know what it is. It's a story tree.

Inside it's dark and beetly – lots of little beetles gnawing away at the cracks and creases in the wood. When I peer out I can see the great branches sweeping the ground, and nothing else, and I know, I just know, that no one would ever find us in here, not raiders, not even the faeries. It's the best hiding place in the world.

'I don't like it,' Peglan says, but everyone hushes her as they crawl inside.

It's a bit cramped, but Ogda sits on Digri, and Peglan sits on Arun till he elbows her off, so she sits on me.

Here we all are then, huddled inside the story tree, and everyone's waiting for me to say something.

I start by telling them the story of the tree.

'A long, long time ago,' I say, pinching Peglan to stop her wriggling, 'the story tree used to be a man. He went from one village to another, telling stories for his supper. One day he knocked on the door of a roundhouse that stood alone, and a woman answered, dressed like an ordinary housewife, but all in green. And she was only three feet tall.

'"Come in," says she, "come in and tell us your tale." But when he looked past her the man could see a great table, spread for a feast, and just one empty place, and all the folk at it staring straight at him.'

I have to push Peglan's head out of the way because her hair keeps getting up my nose. It's dark in the tree, but I can just make out Ogda, her nose running as usual, staring at me as though I've put a spell on her. I love telling stories.

'Then, though he was very hungry, the poor man stood frightened and rooted to the spot with his mouth open, staring, until the woman got angry and said:

> *Rooted as a tree you'll be*
> *No more to tell your own story.*

And before he knew it, the faerie hut had vanished and the little woman along with it. Then the man tried to move and couldn't, for his feet were turning into roots, and his arms to branches. More branches sprang from his shoulders and hair, and he stood alone and fixed and couldn't even cry unless the wind blew.'

'Could he pee?' Arun says, and Digri laughs.

'It'd all turn to sap,' I say sternly. 'But time passed, and the little ash keys fell to the ground, and seedlings grew, and soon the forest grew up around him, swallowing him in. And birds and squirrels and rabbits made their home in him and kept him company. But he can't ever be changed back,' I tell them. 'Not until someone comes who can tell his stories for him.'

Peglan shifts round to look at me, with wide round eyes like Ogda. Digri says, 'Well, that's his hard luck then. 'Cause no one can tell what he's saying.'

'I can,' I say.

'No, you can't.'

'I *can*,' I say, and I make out like I'm listening. And just then the wind moans and Peglan jumps.

'What's he saying now then?' says Arun, like he doesn't believe me.

'He's not saying owt,' says Digri. 'It's the wind!'

'How else is he supposed to speak then?' I say sharply. The great boughs creak again and I hush everyone up. 'He's telling a story,' I say. 'Listen!' And I frown and cup my ear, as though I'll be able to hear it.

'What is it?' cries Peglan, and little Ogda says, 'Tory!'

'It's the story of the Cally Burr,' I tell them. Digri snorts, but he's listening.

'The Cally Burr is a blue-faced hag,' I say, as though repeating the tree's words. 'All summer long she sits by water like a great grey stone, then, on the first day of winter, she comes alive, and goes wailing through the darkness. Water drips from her and she's covered in wet moss and has wet mossy teeth like stones. You can hear her going drip-drip-drip through the forest, looking for children –'

'Why does she?' says Peglan fearfully.

'So she can eat them,' says Arun.

'She needs their blood to turn the berries red,' I tell them. 'And others she gives to the Underworld, so she can stay out of it herself. And then there're the others . . .' I let my voice sink low. 'She turns them into tolly stones.'

I can hear everyone breathing in the crack of the wood, the snuff-snuff-ripple of Ogda's nose, and Peglan breathing through her open mouth.

'They look just like ordinary stones, on the hillside,' I tell them, 'but in the night they move. They creep up on huts, trying to get back to the homes they've lost, reaching out with blind, blunt fingers. And if they touch you – *bam!* – that's it! You're one of them!'

Everyone jumps when I say *bam!* Then, in the darkness of the tree's insides, Arun grabs Peglan's leg, and she screams and kicks and elbows us aside. Then she's off, running as fast as her fat little legs'll carry her, into the heart of the forest, where all paths end.

I swear and scramble out after her, and Digri follows, giving me a look that says *now look what you've done*.

She's disappeared, fast as that. Nothing but trees all around.

'Peglan!' I shout, and the others join in. But now

we're all running in different directions, though Digri's got Ogda clamped to his back.

This'll be like the time I took us all paddling in the river, and Peglan got covered in leeches and wouldn't stop screaming. Or the time I got Digri to eat some different-looking mushrooms and he was sick for a week.

'Peg-lan!' I howl, and hear a sudden scurrying noise, but it's only a squirrel. Then I burst into a clearing and see her, standing absolutely still. I open my mouth to roar, and at the same time see why she's standing still.

A wolf.

Thick shadowy pelt, and eyes like old yellow moons, staring.

None of us moves.

My tongue's stuck rigid in my mouth. All I can see are its eyes, looking at me, not her. Keen and wary, not frightened. Something in them I'll never know.

Maybe the light does it, falling in silver patches around the wolf, but suddenly those eyes aren't wolf eyes any more. More like human eyes, but more wild, more strange than anything human ever got to be. Just for a moment I see myself through those eyes. I can see me, not leaf, not tree, pale and hunted, scared, and I hear its voice in my head. *Keri*, it says, and I can't move.

Then in a quick movement, Digri's bending at my side. He picks up a pine cone and flings it to the far side of the wolf. Arun does the same with a stone from the other direction. The look in the wolf's eyes is startled, still not scared. I can't move, staring back at it. Then, as more pine cones fall around it, the wolf turns, flicking its tail, and pads away, disappearing quickly into shade.

Not hungry then.

I step forward and grab Peglan.

'I seed a wolf!' she says.

'I know you did,' I manage to say. I can still see the eyes of that wolf, but all I can think about is getting back home. And me not getting into trouble. I take her hand and start pulling her along. 'But best not tell anyone, eh? They'll only worry.'

Then of course we can't find the way back. We can't find any of the marks Digri made on the way in; we've run away from them now. We stumble into one clearing after another, and everywhere looks the same. Patches of moonlight fall through the branches, and holes in the tree trunks look like mouths. Don't know how we've stayed in here so long, but the forest is like that. Feels like it's been waiting for this to happen.

'It wasn't my fault,' I say to my mother in my mind.

Digri and Arun want to split up, I think we should stay together, and we all fall out. Then, just as we're getting really worried and grumpy, I hear a voice calling 'Ke-ri! Dig-ri!'

It's Bryn's voice, and Griff's follows. Someone's

banging the calling drum that summons us together at meal times, and I can hear my mother's voice joining in.

'Ke-ri!' she cries, sharp and high. 'Ke-ri!'

We run towards the voices, glad they've found us, even though I'll definitely get into trouble now. Just before we come to them I give Peglan a little shake and say, 'Remember now, don't go talking about wolves!' And she shakes her head solemnly.

Then she sees her mother, who runs towards her with a cry, and she breaks free from me and trots forwards, holding her arms out.

'I seed a wolf!' she cries.

Orla looks horrified. 'A wolf?' she says.

'It weren't any trouble,' says Digri. 'It ran away when we threw cones at it.'

But Peglan's mother is glaring at me. 'She was supposed to look after them!' she says to my mother. 'She does nothing but lead them into trouble! She knows they're not allowed in the forest – they could all have been lost – or – or –'

And she bursts into tears. And Peglan joins in, as though only just realizing that she could have been lost or eaten.

'They're not lost, Orla,' my mother says, mildly enough, though her face is very pale. And Bryn says, 'No harm done,' which is just like him – always trying to keep the peace, and not succeeding.

'No harm?' says Peglan's father, red-faced. 'They've been gone for hours and us all looking for them. Anything could've happened.'

'But it didn't,' Bryn tries again.

'No thanks to her!' Gwern looks as though he would like to hit me. 'How many times have they been told not to wander from the pathways? The others are too little or too daft but she –' he jabs a finger in my direction – 'she is old enough to know better! And you'll let her get away with it – you always do. If she was my daughter she'd have a good whipping!'

And he looks as though he will do it now. My mother takes hold of my shoulders, half rough, half protective. 'She is not your daughter,' she says.

'More's the pity,' says Gwern, but he turns away. 'If Lu were here he would do something about it,' is his parting shot.

Lu was my father. Bryn stares after Gwern, white-lipped. He knows that whatever he does, he does not live up to his brother. My mother steers me towards the huts. 'Come away, Bryn,' she says. 'Leave it. We are all tired.'

And Bryn does as she tells him, as he always does. He will not fight Gwern, and if he did, he would not win. Anyway, he is no fighter. No stomach for it, Myrna says.

One by one we all return to the huts. No one speaks, but I can tell from their faces that their thoughts are like Gwern's. It isn't fair. It was Arun who grabbed Peglan and made her run away, and got us all lost in the first place. We could've found the way back from the story tree. But no one says anything to Arun, and he goes off, sly and dark, into Mabda's hut. Myrna stands there in the doorway, peering out anxiously with her old, blind eyes.

'They are all safe, Mother,' Mabda tells her, and Myrna says, 'Thanks be.'

My footsteps are dragging as they enter our hut. I expect a huge row, but all my mother says is, 'Go to your bed, Keri.'

I want to explain to her, to tell her what happened, and that it wasn't really my fault, or not all of it, anyway, but something in her face forbids it, and I go to bed without any supper. I lie awake a long time, hungry, thinking about the eyes of that wolf, and how it called to me, and knew my name. I can't even think about what my punishment will be in the morning. When I close my eyes I can still see those other eyes, staring, wolf and not-wolf, something looking out at me, through those old yellow eyes.

My punishment is that I have to stay in the hut all day and look after Lu, while the adults work and all the others play. This would be bad enough on an ordinary day, but today is cold and sunny and beautiful. Frost touches the plums and the grass is just starting to crackle. I have to watch while Dillon and Arun and Peglan and Little Ogda are allowed to pick berries.

And Lu is a pain all morning. His right cheek is flushed and my mother says he must be cutting a tooth. Then she says he might have griping pains in his stomach. Whatever it is, he won't play. He strikes at the corn dollies when I hold them out to him and kicks at the scatter-stones. He holds his arms out to be picked up, then, when I pick him up, he pushes me away.

Then he chases all the hens when I try to feed them, and Myrna cackles from the doorway of her hut. 'He was born running, that one,' she says.

Well, he wasn't *born* running, but he learned fast. And to climb in and out of the ditch, and get into the storehouse and knock over all the piles of apples and turnips. And because he has not yet learned to look where he is going, the air is filled with his cries. In just one morning, though I watch him all the time, he falls into the briar patch, and burns himself on our pot, and is run over by our pig.

'Sit *still*, Lu,' I tell him, but he doesn't want to sit still at all, even while I count to five on my fingers. Myrna cackles again and suggests tethering him to a post. I'm tempted, but my mother wouldn't hear of it. So I pick him up and sing to him. And Lu cries and whimpers and tugs at his ear.

'Likely he's teething,' Myrna says. 'He'll be fine when the tooth comes.'

I can hear the sound of Dillon and Arun playing and laughing and splashing further up the river. They have forgotten me already, I think, and tears prick my eyes.

I'm fed up of looking after Lu, and fetching water, and feeding hens and spinning wool, just because I'm a girl.

I wish there was another girl here, my own age, that I could play with.

I hate my ordinary life.

In the afternoon, my mother takes Lu and goes with the other women to scrape lichen from stones for dye. Digri and the others will gather berries for the same purpose. I have to stay with Myrna, helping her.

I can't play in the forest, or by the river. I have to stay in the dim hut all afternoon, mashing berries and spinning wool. I can't even go to the storehouse because that would be going out of her sight. And Myrna is near enough blind.

I argue with Bryn about this at the midday meal, but I don't get anywhere.

'I don't want to go to Myrna,' I say.

'There's nothing you can do here,' says Bryn.

'But I want to stay with you,' I say to my mother. 'I want to help. I can look after Lu.'

'Do you not think you've done enough damage already?' says Bryn, his face dark with anger. 'The best thing you can do is stay out of the way.'

I stare at him, my mouth open, then look at my mother. But she doesn't stand up for me. She turns her face into the shadows. So I push my bowl away and leave.

My steps drag, thinking about Myrna, hating Bryn. He is only angry because of what Gwern said to him, and now he has to prove he can be tough. If Mabb was here now, I think, I would ask her to turn Bryn into a great spotted toad, and watch the heron come and eat him up.

Myrna is sitting in the doorway of her hut as usual. A large dribble of juice runs down her chin, and I wonder how it is that someone who can see everything can't find her own mouth.

'So you have come to keep me company,' she says as I stand in front of her. She waves her hand towards a little stool in the hut behind. 'Sit,' she says.

Myrna holds a distaff and I wind the wool round the spindle over and over, twisting it into thread.

I can hear Digri and Arun and Peglan outside somewhere; the sound of their playing is loud and clear. I shift myself on the little stool, and rub my nose and tell myself it could be worse. At least Lu's with my mother. Myrna says nothing, just leans over the thread until her long nose almost touches it, humming to herself.

After a short while my neck aches, and my nose and eyes are itchy from the wool. It always makes me itch.

'I hate spinning!' I burst out, and Myrna cackles softly.

'You know what happened to the spider who hated spinning?' she says, nodding to where one is hanging from the doorframe, and I wonder how she knows. 'No,' I say sulkily.

'It fell off,' she says, and I can't help laughing.

Then Digri arrives with a basket of berries and stares at me. I make a face at him and he goes away again. Myrna gets up slowly and says, 'Time for mashing.' She cuts the thread I'm holding and hands me the basket. I have to drain the juice into a bowl for dye, and mash the berries for a long time, until they turn into a thick pulp. Myrna sits in the doorway, her face turned to the sky. She grinds seeds into a paste that we will bake in the fire later on, but she chews just as many as she grinds.

No one knows how old Myrna is. Mabda is her daughter, and she already seems old. And no one knows where Myrna came from. My mother said that she was a little girl when the People found her, separated from her clan. A little wild girl, dressed in skins.

And whether her people had all died in the hard winter no one knew, but they never came back for her. She couldn't talk, except in animal noises. She could growl like a dog and bay like a wolf, or grunt like a pig, and the animals understood her and she understood them. And she could do magic. She could draw out the shape of the land in the dirt with a stick, and track wild deer for a hundred miles by scent alone. When she called down the rain it came.

Her people didn't live in huts, my mother said, but followed their animals around, like we used to in the First Days. And it's true that Myrna does not like to be inside. She sits always at the doorway of her hut, even on the coldest day, chewing her herbs into a paste and spitting them out again. She uses the paste to heal our wounds or keep off illness, and she uses her stories, she says, to heal our spirits.

At last, when my arms and neck are one long ache, the pulp sets so that Myrna can cut it with a knife and lay strips of it on a flat stone. When it has dried hard it will be ready to store for the winter – a little strip of summer sun to see us through the cold and dark.

'It will be a long dark, this year,' Myrna says, following my thought again. 'In two or three days the first rains will come, then the winds. Then the long rains will begin.'

I don't ask her how she knows. That's another of

44

the gifts she brought from her people to ours. She can sniff the weather for days to come. Because of her we began storing food early. Beans and turnips and garlic are gathered into the storehouse with barley and other grains, and soon another pig will be slaughtered. I hope it isn't ours – the pig I have fed from my own plate, who has pushed her warm snout into my hands and given us three piglets. But so much food is needed to see the People through the freezing nights.

Myrna hands me another basket of berries and I sigh gustily and sit down again, thinking about Digri and Arun and Peglan and Ogda gathering them and playing on the edge of the forest.

'You would rather be out there, eh?' she says, looking at me keenly with those sightless eyes. I would rather be outside anywhere, hunting for bird's eggs, gathering sticks for the fire, than indoors. She knows because she was just like me. When she was my age, she had no home, only the herd.

'What was it like then?' I ask her suddenly. She knows what I mean.

'It was no different,' she tells me. 'There was wind, and rain and snow. The ground was as hard then as it is now, and the forest as dark.'

But I want to know more. 'Tell me about the magic, Myrna,' I ask her.

'Humphh,' she says scornfully, spitting seed.

'My mother says you could fly.'

'Hrrummph!' says Myrna, spitting some more. It's not the answer I was hoping for.

'Can I do magic?' I ask her. 'Can you teach me?'

'What do you want to do magic for? You want to fly like a bird and swim like a fish?' she says, and I nod eagerly.

'Maybe the bird looks at you and thinks, *I wish I was like her.*'

I snort. 'I don't think so,' I say.

'Why not?'

I stare at her. 'I can't fly, I can't swim underwater, I can't tunnel for miles under the earth. I can't do anything!'

'You can watch and learn and hear things in your mind. You can dream, and paint the dream on to a wall. You can weave baskets.'

'That's not magic,' I say.

'Magic has many forms,' says Myrna. 'It's nothing separate. It's the wind in the night and the dust on the path. It's the moss on a stone and the shadow of a cloud.'

But they're just the ordinary things. That's not what I mean by magic. I frown, not understanding.

'But Mabb's real,' I say.

'Real as you and me. Realer, some might say. Longer I live, the more I don't think we're real at all. Only the magic.'

46

I'm getting confused by all this. I try again.

'Have you seen Mabb?' I say.

'I've seen her,' she says. 'And so have you.'

'No, I haven't.'

Myrna snorts again. 'No use being able to see, if you don't know what you're looking at.'

I'm silent then because I don't know what she means. Then I start thinking about the wolf in the forest. What would it be like to stare into the forest through those yellow eyes? Would it look like the forest I see? I try to imagine it now, hunched over my basket of slimy berries, and all at once I can see a different, wilder forest, tangled at root level, full of shade and patches of light. Every rustle, every movement means something. Just like the wolf, I can see the forest staring back at me. Then in a moment, everything shifts, and I am the eyes of the forest, and it's looking through me.

Keri, it says.

'Keri?' says Myrna, bringing me back with a jolt. She's looking at me with her head cocked to one side. 'Where've you gone to?' she asks, but I can't answer. I look around the hut, surprised to find I'm still here. Firelight dancing on the pots and Myrna's grey plaits swinging near my face.

'You'll be falling into them berries,' she says. 'Time to weave some baskets.'

She drains the last juice from the berries into a

47

bowl, and puts a handful of rushes into it and swishes them around. Then she shows me a basket she's been weaving – half finished with the stems of rushes sticking out from it like the rays of the sun. She pulls up a stool to the door and we both sit by the doorway. Afternoon light slants in.

Myrna hands me a plain, undyed stem and shows me how to weave it in and out of the dyed ones, so that the colours mingle and twine, spreading outwards.

'Like seeds growing,' she says, and I remember that every basket she weaves tells a story.

'Will you tell me a story?' I ask her.

'What kind of a story?' Myrna says.

'About Mabb,' I say, and Myrna shoots me a look.

'What about her?' she says.

'Well . . .' I have to put my question carefully. 'If you wanted to find her, where would you look?'

Myrna pegs up a rope, so that we can hang the coloured rushes on it.

'You don't go looking for Mabb,' she says. 'She comes looking for you, if she wants you.'

I wish she would, I think, but I don't say it.

Myrna hears me anyway. 'You don't know what you're wishing for,' she says, very stern. I look away from her, and start weaving my rushes. No matter how I try, I can't weave them as tightly as Myrna.

Myrna settles herself back on her stool and says,

'She doesn't look the same, Mabb, not two times running. She comes when you least expect her, and she looks like the thing you least expect. You've probably seen her every day, but you don't know how to look.'

I look up at her then, squinting earnestly through the sun. 'Tell me,' I beg.

Myrna glares at me with her filmy eyes. 'Haven't I told you already?' she says. 'Don't all my stories tell you how dangerous she is? I've told you, many times, but you don't hear.'

It seems like a cold shadow has fallen between us, over my heart. I remember the moths by the water-lily pond, and the wolf. 'I do,' I tell her.

It's not that I think Mabb isn't dangerous – she is – dangerous and wild and beautiful. I don't know why I would want to see her; I can't explain it. But without all that danger, without the wildness, life is just so – ordinary. Sometimes I just want something to *happen*.

Myrna's looking at me with her lips pressed together. 'Like putting your hand in the fire,' she says, and I hang my head. Then she nods to herself and sighs, as though blowing the past away.

'Tell me a story anyway,' I say timidly.

Myrna grunts. 'Too many stories,' she says. But then she begins.

'A long time ago,' she says, 'a woman of the People gave birth to a beautiful baby boy.'

Lu, I think. He is the most beautiful of all the little

49

ones. Not Ogda with her plain, screwed-up face. Not Derry, who is a great fat baby who hardly moves.

'He was so beautiful, the woman feared that the faeries would grow jealous and steal him. She wouldn't leave him or set him down, but bound him to her with strips of cloth. She'd already lost her husband, you see, and the baby was all she had.'

'How?' I say, interrupting.

'What?'

'How did she lose her husband?'

Myrna glares at me. 'Them that listens, finds out,' she says. And she nods at my basket, meaning I should get on with it.

'One night a great storm blew up. It rattled all the pots on the table and blew out the fire. The woman sat in her chair, holding her baby, and singing songs to calm him because he was restless.

'All night the storm raged. The wind moaned and there was the sound of branches scratching the walls of the hut. The woman was feared for she knew that the forest had crept up around them, its wet branches slapping the walls. Then the river rose up and pressed its mouth against the windows.

'"Give the child to us," it moaned.

'"Go away!" cried the woman. "You will never have him." And as soon as she said this, a blast of wind blew the door right open. The woman leapt up and put the baby in his cot to keep him warm while she

50

pressed the door back and shut out the water that was streaming through. She could see that the little hut was entirely surrounded by forest and river – all the other huts had disappeared.

'When she turned back to the room, Mabb was there, holding the baby and smiling. Her eyes were like rain on the river, and her gown ended in pools of water on the floor.

'"I will keep him safe," she said.

'"No!" cried the woman. "He is mine!"

'"You can have more children," Mabb said. "I want this one."

'The woman fell to her knees. "Please!" she begged. "Please don't take my baby!"

'Mabb looked at her with eyes like frost on stone. "What can you give this child?" she asked. "Sickness and hunger will come. In one year, maybe two, he will be lying in the cold earth. Is that what you want for him?"

'The woman sobbed aloud and Mabb touched her cheek. "If he comes with me," she said, "neither sickness nor grief nor pain will hurt him. The rain will not touch him, nor the wind chill. What can you give him compared to that?"

'The woman raised her face to Mabb's. "Love," she said.

'For a moment Mabb's face flickered fierce as lightning. "I will love him," she said.

'Then the woman wept. She tried to clutch Mabb's skirts, but they slipped through her fingers like rain. She begged Mabb over and over not to take her baby.

'Mabb stood, tall and terrible. Then she said, "We will see about your mortal love. If you can keep watch over this child for three days and nights, you may keep him. But mind, you must not take your eyes off him, or he is mine."

'Before the woman could speak, Mabb raised her hand, and the room shifted around her, then she was gone.

'The woman blinked. The child lay in its cot, sleeping peacefully. A cold blast of air rattled the door. Without thinking, the woman moved to shut it. Then she remembered with a pang of fear, and ran to her baby and bound him to her with strips of cloth. And in that way she did all the tasks of the house, raking the fire, boiling the porridge. Then she sat in her chair with the baby at her breast, and rocked and murmured him back to sleep, though she did not dare to sleep herself. And so the first night passed.

'The second night was much harder. The woman could hardly keep her eyes open. She chewed bitter herbs to keep herself awake. The baby cried and she fed him. He grew fretful, strapped to her breast, so she put him in his cradle and stood over him, her head nodding and jolting up again. And so the second night passed.

'But by the third day she felt like she was in a dark dream, neither waking nor sleeping. She even began to think she'd dreamed Mabb and the promise she'd made. As she fed the baby her head nodded forward, so she stood up once more and put him back in his cot.

'The wind murmured at her through the chinks in the wall. "Help me, dear wife," said her husband's voice, and she ran overjoyed to the door, for she hadn't seen her husband since before the baby was born, since the day he'd left to go hunting. She flung the door open but there was nothing there. Terror struck her, and when she turned back to the cot there was only a turnip's grinning head, wrapped in a blanket.

'The woman cried aloud in grief and fear, but there was only the rattling of the wind and hail. Then she picked up the turnip head in its blanket and said:

> *Turnip head, turnip head,*
> *Lying in my baby's bed,*
> *Tell me where you came from.*

And the turnip head spoke to her and said:

> *Through the gates of the wind and the door of the rain,*
> *On the journey of stones, and back again.*

Then the woman wrapped another blanket round her, and, taking only a short knife for protection, she set

53

off with the turnip child in her arms and her face turned into the wind and rain.'

Myrna breaks off there, getting up stiffly from her stool.

'What happened?' I ask her.

But Myrna only says, 'Are you hungry?' And I realize I am. Myrna takes the paste she made from the seeds and shapes it into rough circles. She bakes them on a flat stone on the fire, while I carry on trying to weave my basket. I'm desperate to hear the rest of the story, but I know Myrna won't be rushed. She dribbles some honey over the little cakes, then I put the basket down, and we eat them in the doorway, and they taste good in the cold sun.

'Did the woman find her baby?' I ask, with my mouth full.

'The wind and the rain grew worse,' Myrna says, just as if she'd never stopped speaking, and crumbs catch in the bristles on her chin. 'But the woman turned her face into them and battled on. She hadn't gone very far when she came to a pond. The water in it was all whipped up by the wind and rain. The woman looked at her reflection, all broken up in the water, and said, "How unhappy I am."

'Then the water writhed and churned and a great fish rose out of it. It was spotted and spiny and it opened its great fishy mouth and said:

Unhappy may you be,
You are not so unhappy as me.

The woman was terrified, and started to run away, but the turnip head said:

Cut the fish from gill to fin,
Flay it open and keep the skin.

The woman was horrified, but she did as she was told, trying not to look at the great fishy eyes, or hear its gurgling breath. But when she'd finished, an old woman stepped from the skin, brown-spotted and bristly with age.

'"Queen Mabb changed me because I would not bring babies to her," she said. "Now you have set me free. Take the fish skin when you pass through the door of the rain."

'The woman thanked her as she rolled the fish skin lightly, and it folded until it was hardly there. Then she tucked it into the neck of her gown and carried on, turning her face once more into the rain.

'She walked and walked on a stony road. Stones filled her shoes and the rain battered her and made her wet clothes cling, but she didn't stop. And after a long time she came to a place where four roads met, and at the point where they crossed there was a thorn tree, and trapped in the thorn tree was a great black bird. And the bird cawed:

> *Woe is me, woe is me,*
> *I am trapped upon this tree,*
> *Who will come to set me free?*

The woman looked at the turnip head, but the turnip head said nothing. So she put it down, then took her knife and set about the thorns. They tore at her cruelly, and ripped her hands, but at last the bird was free.

'It tumbled rather than flew to the ground, because its wings were torn. Then it pecked at the thorns that still stuck to its flesh and said, "Queen Mabb said I should stay until a wood had grown around me. All because I would not hunt for her, or bring her nuts and berries. Now you have set me free. What can I do for you?"

'The woman picked up the turnip head and felt it jiggle in her arms. She turned a little away from the bird and the head said:

> *Wring its neck and roast its feathers.*
> *Then we'll pass through stormy weather.*

'Oh, the poor bird!' I cry, interrupting Myrna. She only glares at me, then carries on as if I haven't spoken.

'What else could the woman do? She went to the bird and it didn't try to get away. She wrung its neck quickly, then made a fire and roasted it until every last black feather fell off. The turnip head told her to weave them into a cloak so she did. And as soon as she draped the cloak around her, a great wind blew up. The woman was tossed and buffeted one way then another, and soon she was lifted completely off her feet. She flew into the wind in her cloak of feathers, and felt the earth rushing away from her, until she came to a place where the sky itself seemed to open, like a gateway. Through this she flew, and landed in a place where no wind ever blew, but the rain fell steadily.

'So much rain fell that the land around her seemed to be dissolving, and the air itself turning to water. The turnip head jiggled in her arms.

'"The fish skin, the fish skin!" it cried, and the woman slipped the fish skin on. She could feel it clinging to her, and she writhed and leapt into the water, swimming through the shimmering rain.

'She swam and swam, until the sky, heavy with rain, pressed down on the water that was covering the earth. It was so heavy that she thought it would crush her, but a little way ahead she could see an opening in the rain, like a doorway, and she leapt through, and lay on dry land.

'She wriggled out of the fish skin and stood up.

57

Behind her were the curtains of rain, before her was a silvery world of starlight and moon-whitened trees. The trees stood around her in a ring, white flowers formed a circle at her feet and even the stars above seemed to shine down in a circle. Then the turnip jiggled in her arms once more.

Set me down, set me down,
Bring to me my faerie crown.

The woman looked but she couldn't see a crown. So she began to weave one from the white flowers, and before she had finished, Mabb appeared before her.

"'Why have you come here?" Mabb said.

"'I have come for my son," the woman said. "See – here is your baby."

'Mabb walked all the way around the turnip head, frowning.

"'That is not my baby," she said. "Do not play tricks on me. That is only the head of a turnip."

'Then the woman dropped the crown of flowers on to the turnip head, and immediately it began crying like a baby.

"'Yes, he is my baby, I see it now," Mabb said, and she picked him up. Then there was another cry, and the woman's own baby lay where the turnip head had been. She picked him up gladly, and immediately

Mabb and the turnip head, and the land around them, disappeared, and the woman stood once more at the crossroads with the thorn tree and the charred remains of the bird she had roasted.

'A few black feathers still clung to her, so she plucked them off and dropped them on to the bird by way of saying thank you. But as soon as they fell, the bird began to move and change shape, and her husband stepped from the ashes of the fire.

'"I was hunting for food when Mabb came to me," he said, "and asked me for the food I had gathered. But when I would not give it to her, she changed me, and trapped me in the tree. Then you came and set me free."

'And so at last they made their way home together, and were never parted again.'

I'm quiet when Myrna finishes her tale. I know it's only a story, but I can't help thinking about my father, and how he went away. *Maybe he isn't dead, after all*, I'm thinking. *Maybe Mabb knows where he is.* I can see the four of us together, my mother and father, me and Lu, and there's a kind of light around us all so that for a moment I have to blink very hard.

I don't say any of this to Myrna, who is gazing into the far distance.

'What happened to Mabb?' I ask.

'What do you mean?' says Myrna.

'Didn't she ever come back? For the baby.'

'How would I know?' says Myrna irritably. 'It's only a story.'

'Mabb was cruel,' I say slowly. 'What she did was wrong. Didn't they punish her?'

'How would they punish her?' Myrna says. 'Magic is neither cruel nor wrong. It's only magic.'

Only magic, I think. The words echo strangely in my mind. I'm still trying to put my next question together when Mabda arrives, carrying Lu under one arm and holding a pot full of warm milk in the other. Lu wriggles and squawks when he sees me, so I take him off Mabda and he laughs and pats my cheek.

'Working hard?' Mabda says to me, smiling.

'She'll do,' says Myrna. Mabda says that my mother will be back soon, but she has sent Lu back because he keeps running away. 'Can he stay with you till she gets back?' she asks.

'Of course he can,' says Myrna. 'We need some water, though, for the dye.'

'I'll go,' I say, and before anyone can stop me, I scoop up a water bowl with one hand, and hurry out of the hut, still holding Lu in the other.

Of course, I'm not supposed to leave the huts but I'm tired of staying in. My legs are aching from sitting still all afternoon. I'm not supposed to take Lu to the river either, but I reckon I can be there and back before anyone notices.

I go a different way to the river, to avoid seeing my

mother or Bryn, and I kneel down and dip the bowl into the water. It's one of Myrna's most tightly woven baskets, made of reeds dyed with different-coloured lichens and braided together so no water escapes. No one else can weave a bowl so cunningly that it doesn't leak, and so that the patterns are beautiful and each one means something. This one has something to do with the flight of swans, and in the water, where the colours ripple and change, I can see their movement. I lean over and touch them through the water. *They are flying to Mabb*, I think. If I could follow them, I might find my father. Just like the woman found her husband and baby, in Myrna's story.

But of course I have to let go of Lu's hand, just for a moment, and when I look up again he isn't there.

'Lu!' I shout, then I stand up, blowing all my breath out at once. 'Lu?'

Nothing. I'm scared now, not angry.

'Lu – stop it!' I shout. 'Come back now!'

Then I hear a dull splash, like a large stone hitting the water, and I run towards it, crying in my mind. *Oh, Lu, sweet baby brother, don't fall in the river, baby – don't fall in Lu, please, PLEASE!*

I see his brown curls bobbing in the water, and throw myself in after them without stopping to think.

The river pulls me in. It's strong and terrible. It

seizes my whole body. I struggle to hold my head up, and flap my arms and kick. My tunic's all tangled up with my legs, and when I try to shout *Lu!*, water gushes into my mouth. The river drags my head under as I lunge towards Lu. Then I've got him, but he's still face down and I can't turn his head round. The water is pulling and pushing both of us downstream, and I can't do anything about it. I can't get us both to the bank.

No one knows where we are. No one can hear if I scream for help. The water roars in my ears and tugs at us, stronger and stronger. I'm kicking hard, but the water's stronger than my legs. I bump my hip on a huge stone, and try to hold on, but the water tears me away. I feel as though it will tear me in two. I let go of the rock and I'm sucked under. It's cold. The coldness soaks into me. I push my head up again, spluttering, and we're whirled along, rolling and tossing like willow branches.

The river isn't playing. It's strong and terrible and never stopping. It's roaring in my head and I can't feel anything any more. I can't even feel if I'm still holding Lu. This isn't what I meant when I wanted something to happen – if I lose Lu, I'll be in trouble for the rest of my life!

Suddenly I can hear someone shouting and I don't even know if it's me. My head's sucked under again, and I force it up, spluttering. Then a branch thrusts towards me, and Bryn's face is shouting something I can't hear. I grab hold of the branch and the water sucks me under again. There's a great splash as someone else leaps in. I feel something tugging Lu away from me and I let go, but I'm still gripping the branch. The water pulls at me and pushes too, trying to drag my head under the branch, but my chin grips on to it and my arm clutches. All I can feel is that branch, scraping my chin, and the river, tugging me away. Can't feel my fingers, but they're slipping, slipping. Then I feel the branch moving sideways, against the tug of the river, and I bump against the bank.

Bryn hauls me out. From the corner of my eye, I see that Arval's got Lu and is pumping the water out of him. I'm terrified that he's dead, but I can't speak. I close my eyes and feel the earth under me. I lie on it and all I can do is breathe. The ground is hard and solid and it doesn't move.

'Lu,' I say, when I can speak.

'Can you get up?' Bryn says.

When I try to move, my head whirls. Then I feel Bryn's hands under my arms, hauling me upwards. All my clothes cling to me, and I try to ask if Lu's all right, but my teeth start to chatter and my legs buckle when I take a step.

Bryn picks me up. I see the stones and the earth banked up where they're building the dyke. Arval carries Lu and Bryn carries me, almost running back up the hill towards the huts. Griff and Gwern are staring, but I can't look at them. I can't look at anyone. My head is still filled with the roaring of the river. I turn my face into Bryn's shirt and bump and jerk against his chest as he carries me.

Then my mother comes running. 'What's happened?' she cries. She takes a look at my face, then tries to take Lu from Arval, but he walks past her. She runs with us, all the way to our hut.

Bryn puts me down, and I can stand now, holding on to the wall. Arval finally hands Lu to my mother. Lu's head lolls backwards and his face is green.

'He's swallowed a lot of water,' Arval says.

Bryn and Arval make up a little bed near the fire, and my mother kneels down on it, clutching Lu. Lu coughs and turns his face away.

He's alive! I think, and relief gushes into me like water. I take a few steps forward and sink down on the bed near my mother. No one looks at me. My mother is still holding Lu, with a strange, terrible look in her eyes. Bryn nods at Arval, and he leaves.

'What happened?' he says.

I try to explain what happened – that I only took my eyes off Lu for one minute – that I only took him down to the river in the first place because I didn't want to let him out of my sight. It's the best story I can come up with but none of it comes out right. Lu lies pale and still and my mother chews her lip. Then finally she turns to me, but all she says is, 'Take your wet things off, Keri.' Then she looks away from me and will not look back. I stare at her, and try to speak, but she only bends over Lu, whispering.

I go into my room and peel all my wet things off. I don't have anything else to wear, so I stay where I am, only peering round the sackcloth hanging to see what's happening.

My mother makes up a thick brew in a pot. She rubs Lu's chest with a mixture of feverfew and garlic, and the bitter scent fills the air. Then she takes some of the herbs she's mixed into a paste and puts them on Lu's tongue. It makes him splutter and cough again, but she keeps on doing it, and suddenly he's sick. A great flow of greenish water spills over her hand and on to the bed.

More people come to the doorway of our hut. Tilse is there, then Griff, and I can see Gwern pressing behind.

'How is the boy?' Griff asks. No one asks about me.

My mother doesn't answer him. She glances over to where I stand, half wrapped in the sackcloth curtain. 'Pass your wet things through, Keri,'

She's still not looking at me properly, but I hurry to do as she asks. I pass my wet clothes through the curtain, Bryn takes them from me and my mother drapes them on some sticks near the fire. I catch Griff looking at me.

'Wasn't she supposed to be looking after him?'

My mother comes over to me and takes my leggings from me. I look urgently up into her face. 'Mother – I didn't –' I begin. But her face is terrible – stern and far away at the same time.

'It's a good job we were by the river,' Griff says, still looking at me.

I turn away then. I don't want him to talk to me while I'm standing here naked. Besides, it's cold. I lie down on my mattress and pull the cover over me. My hip hurts where I banged it on the rock, so I can only lie on one side. I want to show my mother the bruise, but she's too busy with Lu.

I hear Myrna saying, 'We'll see how he is in the morning.' Then I can hear people leaving.

When I close my eyes all I can see is the river. I can still hear it roaring in my ears. I try to get warm in my bed, to stop shivering. I'm in real trouble now. But no one thinks of how I jumped in after him, and wouldn't let go. My ears strain towards my mother and Bryn, to hear if they're talking about me, but I can't hear anything. I close my eyes again, remembering all the times I played by the river, with Digri and Arun and Peglan and little Ogda, making necklaces out of reeds and laughing as the fat frogs plopped into the water.

Seemed like a different river then.

I try to stay awake, worrying about Lu, and about what my punishment will be, but I can't. Sleep pulls me downwards, closing over my face like water.

In the night I'm woken up by Lu's crying, a thin, high, tearing sound. It's hard to sleep with your fingers stuffed in your ears. After a few moments I can't stand it any more, and I kneel up and peek through the curtain.

There is my mother, pale and red-eyed, holding Lu against her shoulder, and his head's turning this way and that. Bryn's stirring something in the pot, and there's a bitter smell. The fire's smoking badly, and it stings my eyes. I duck down again quickly before they catch me looking, because I know I'm in trouble. Feel all hollow inside. Stuff my fingers back in my ears. I hold on to my father's amulet and whisper,

'Stop screaming, stop screaming,' over and over.

Nothing happens, of course. After a moment I peek through the curtain once more. There's only a sliver of light from the moon at the window, but I can see my mother putting Lu in the cradle. He kicks and thrashes, then bawls like a lost calf. Bryn says something and my mother answers him sharply. Then she picks Lu up again, rocking him forwards and back, and Bryn leaves.

'Mam?' I whisper, then I have to say it louder. 'Mam?'

She barely glances my way. 'Go to sleep, Keri.'

But I'm wide awake now. I pull the cover round me and slip out, greatly daring. Then I crouch at her side and bury my face in her and breathe in her smell, which is the smell of honey and sweat and smoke, from tending the fire. She doesn't hug me or even pat my hair, and after a moment I look up. 'Where's Bryn?' I say.

'Gone to fetch Myrna,' she says, then I know it must be serious. No one goes for Myrna in the middle of the night, unless it's life or death. I feel a sharp pang of fear. 'How's Lu?' I say. I kneel up, so that I can see him better, and my mother lays him in her lap. One side of his face is swollen and red.

'Lu?' I say timidly, but he doesn't respond. Only one side of his face screws up when he cries. His eyelids flutter, but he's not properly awake. My stomach twists. Seems like he's far away, somewhere I can't follow.

I wish I could see his eyes, which are big and greenish, like my father's eyes. Only in the left one there is a brown freckle. I put out a finger and touch his fine hair, that's clinging to his forehead with sweat.

'What's wrong with him?' I ask, but my mother doesn't answer. She tucks a strand of her hair behind her ear. Seems like she's gone far away from me too. I tug at her sleeve and she looks at me then for the first time, her face half shaded by the fire. Then she puts out a hand and touches my cheek.

'Mam – I didn't mean to let him go!' I whisper urgently. 'I only let go of him to dip my basket in the water – and I jumped in to save him!'

She doesn't say it's my fault, for taking him to the river in the first place, and letting him fall in. Her fingers run from my face to my hair and back again, then down my neck to the amulet, and she manages the ghost of a smile.

I know what she's thinking. She's told me the story many times. My father carved it from the antler of a deer, to drive evil spirits away, and wouldn't speak to anyone while he carved it, so that all the power he could summon would go into this one magic charm. To keep me safe.

'He spent all one morning whittling it,' she tells me now. 'It was after . . .' But her voice trails away as we hear other voices outside.

Myrna's long shadow fills the room, and I rise and stand silently by my mother.

Crookbacked though she is, Myrna is very tall, and she looks about her with those sightless eyes.

'Show me the child,' she says.

My mother rises and takes Lu to Myrna, then Bryn fetches the stool and Myrna sits on it, putting Lu on her lap. He twists and whimpers restlessly. Her long fingers probe him this way and that.

'Has he a rash?' she asks.

In fact he does have a rash, when my mother pulls his shirt up. A little rash, like strawberries under his skin. Myrna clucks and shakes her head. Then she prods the swollen place beneath his ear.

'Poison in there,' she says. 'It'll have to be drawn.'

My mother and Bryn look at one another. 'Poison?' says my mother, her voice catching. 'It can't be − I mean −' She looks helplessly at Bryn.

I can see them thinking, *this is no ordinary sickness.*

Myrna's chewing something, and her face works strangely. I look from Myrna, to Lu, then my mother, until Myrna says, 'Heat the knife.'

Bryn's hovering behind my mother, his face pale, but he turns to the fire. I see the glint of the short blade in the flames. Feels like my voice is all stopped up in my throat. My mother's face is greyish, sagging with fear. She takes Lu from Myrna and lays him on the little bed that's made up by the fire, cupping his head in her hands.

Stiffly, Myrna drops to her knees. Then Bryn hands her the knife. Suddenly I find my voice.

'NO!' I say.

Myrna barely glances at me, but my mother looks up, white-lipped.

'Go to bed, Keri,' she says, in a trembling voice. But I fling myself forwards as though I will throw myself over Lu's body.

'Don't let her!' I say. 'Don't let her cut him!'

'Keri!' says my mother, very stern, and I can feel Bryn's hand on my shoulder. But I wrench away from him. 'Don't let her!' I cry. I turn to Myrna. 'Stay away from him!' I shout at her, and my mother gasps.

Myrna's face is still as carved stone, waiting. Bryn pulls me back.

'Come away, Keri,' he says.

All my words shrivel in my mouth as he hauls me upwards. I take one step back, then another. The short blade flashes as Myrna lifts it, then lowers it to his neck. Lu's body goes rigid, arched. Then he squeals, a high-pitched, terrible squeal, and suddenly I can't stand it any more. I push past Bryn and run to my bed, flinging myself down on it and stuffing my fingers in my ears the way I did when Griff and Gwern killed the hog.

These were all the children of my father's house.

One before me that died, a boy.

One after me that died, a girl.

Two that came early and never drew breath.

Another boy, that died in the Year of Sickness.

And Lu.

But Lu can't die, he mustn't die!

Sweet Lu, sweet helpless baby brother. Why did I let you go?

My fingers are stuck so hard in my ears that I can hear the blood pounding in my head. Even that doesn't shut out the sound of him screaming.

I remember the time Myrna cut an abscess from my knee. I was sick with the pain – I thought I would die of it. And Lu is only a baby.

With that thought, the tears come. And with them, the shame of hiding in my room. I take my fingers from my ears – just in time to hear Lu's howling drain away into a choking rattle.

Slowly, afraid of what I might see, I make my way back to the sackcloth hanging. Myrna, my mother and Bryn are all crouched over Lu. I step into the room.

Lu is lying pale and still, his eyes rolled back in his head so that I can only see two crescent moons of white.

'What have you done to him?' I ask hoarsely, but no one answers. My mother's mopping yellowish fluid from his neck. Myrna's packing the cut with whatever she's been chewing in her mouth. Lu is so quiet and still, the redness in his cheek replaced by a bluish hollow.

He looks like my father looked, before he died.

Come back, I want to call to him, but my voice won't work. I remember all the times he has slept in my arms, and how his face lights up when he sees me, and how he laughs, all gum, when I tickle him, and how when I hide my face in my hands, then open them again, his face breaks into a smile of pure joy, all because I'm there.

My mother's eyes are red with weeping. I look up at her, but she doesn't look at me, and neither does Bryn. It's as though I'm not there.

Lu seems so far away, I don't know where he is.

'He is travelling where the bird does not fly,' Myrna says, just as if she's heard me thinking. She places a bony hand on my shoulder. 'Where the fish cannot swim, nor the wolf follow.'

I stare at her. She is talking about the Underworld, where the dead go.

'But he will come back,' I say. 'Can't you bring him back?'

'No one can bring him back,' she says, and my stomach twists in fear.

'Why not?' I whisper.

Myrna rises stiffly from her stool. 'He must decide whether to come back,' she says.

'But – we have to do something!' I say.

'No, we don't,' she says sternly. 'There is nothing to do.'

I want to hit her then; I want to cry.

'Go to bed, Keri,' Bryn says at last. 'You can't do anything for him.'

But I want to do something, I cry silently. I want to pick him up and hold him. My mother clears away the cloth she used to mop the fluid, and the knife. I want her to speak to me, but she can't talk.

My fingers find the amulet at my throat. I trace the bony shape with my finger and hear my mother's voice saying, 'He spent all one morning whittling it. It was after . . .'

After the other baby died, I finish for her.

My fingers are clasping my amulet, then suddenly I take it off. My breath catches a little as I pull it past my hair. I lean over Lu's cradle. I slip the amulet over his head, so that it rests on his heart. His head is clammy and lolls against my fingers, but he doesn't wake up. Not even his breathing changes. I trace the shape of the charm with my finger.

'Help him, Mabb,' I whisper, and an owl hoots as though in answer. If Mabb was here now, I think suddenly, I would beg her to make Lu well.

Then Myrna is bending over my brother again, smearing something on his lips, and a sweet smell rises. Honey, mixed with herbs.

I stand very still, understanding suddenly. Myrna can do magic with honey. She uses it on wounds, or as a poultice for sore chests. Or, when all hope is passed, she smears it on the lips of the dying, to sweeten their last breath.

'What are you doing?' I cry, seizing her bony arm.

Myrna shakes me off, but I scratch her so that she hisses sharply. 'Leave him alone!' I shout at her, gripping the side of the cot.

There is Lu, pale, unmoving, with the honey smeared on his lips.

I can't believe it – I won't.

I close my eyes. *Mabb!* I call silently. *Take me, not Lu!*

There is no answer to this, though I think the thought three times and send it out with all the force I can summon, like an arrow from the bow. But when I open my eyes there's no change in him, no change at all. His face is still mottled by the rash and sunken, somehow – bluish shadows beneath his eyes. I stare and stare at him, hoping to find some sign of change, then this strange thought comes to me, that he doesn't look like my brother any more. It's almost as if another baby lies there, like Lu and not like him. He is shrunken somehow, and wizened.

'Where is he?' I say suddenly. Then, 'What have you done to him?'

'Keri,' my mother says sharply, and Bryn says, 'That's enough.'

'What have you done with him?' I say.

My mother comes to me then and clasps my face with her cold hands. 'He has to go now,' she says, nodding at me. But her eyes are strange – like two wells with all the water in them frozen at the bottom.

'No!' I say, pulling away from her. I start to back

away, still staring at the shrivelled body in the cot. I can't believe that it is Lu. I go on staring at Lu who is not Lu, and suddenly it comes to me so clearly I almost laugh.

'It isn't Lu,' I say, pointing. 'That – that thing – it isn't him!'

'Keri!' says my mother, shocked, and Myrna says, 'You don't know what you are saying, child.'

'Look – look at it!' I cry. 'That isn't Lu – it isn't even like him!' I'm babbling now, desperate to make them see what I see.

'Don't talk nonsense,' Bryn says. 'Who else would it be?'

'It isn't Lu!' I say, shaking my head. 'It isn't – it isn't!'

'Keri!' My mother is angry now. 'Do not talk so wildly!'

'But it isn't him!' I cry. I clutch at Myrna. 'Tell them – tell them it isn't him. He's been changed – like the story – tell them he's a changeling!'

A murmur rises from the doorway, and for the first time I realize that everyone is clustered there. I can see Tilse's face, and Gwern.

'Changeling!' someone says, but Myrna is unmoved.

'Peace, child,' she says, very stern.

'I know my own brother!' I shout. 'And that isn't him! Mabb has taken him!'

A stir ripples through everyone at the doorway, and my mother's face twists with anger, pain and fear.

'How dare you say it's not Lu!' she hisses, gripping my shoulders. 'Look at him! You have done this! This would never have happened if you hadn't taken him to the river! Look at what you have done'

I stare at her with tears in my eyes. 'But it isn't him!' I say. 'Mabb has taken him – just like she took my father!'

I say no more, for my mother slaps me so hard my head rings. I'm too shocked to cry. I stare at her and her face is white with rage.

'Your father is dead,' she says in low, terrible tones. 'Get away from me. Get out of my sight!'

She is so angry she doesn't look like my mother at all. She looks like a demon who will slap me again, but Bryn holds her back.

All the words I have to say are jammed in my throat and I can't move. Then suddenly I'm running, smacking into people at the doorway, past Digri and Ogda, and Arun and Peglan, who are pressing in behind the others. They stare at me, open mouthed, as I run, but all I can think of is my brother, and Mabb who has taken him, and how I have to get him back. My chest hurts as I stumble up the hill, running faster and faster towards the forest.

PART II

Sun's shining. That's the first thing I notice when I open my eyes. I shut them again quickly, then squint upwards, through layers and layers of leaves.

Shadows of leaves move over my face. I turn then, and squint into the green of tree roots and ivy. Must've fallen asleep in the forest. Don't know how that happened. Nothing hurt me, though. I've not been eaten by wild beasts, nor sucked into a swamp.

I sit up slowly, feeling bruised. My head hurts. Don't even know where I am.

Forest is quiet – that's one thing. Just goes to show that it's not as dangerous as people tell you. Can't believe I've spent a full night here, though. No one else has. Or if they did, they didn't come back. I feel a prick of pride when I think of everyone's faces as I tell them my story. *Yes there were wolves, and bears and raiders – but they didn't bother me.*

Something's hurting, though. There's a pain in my foot. I sit back and look at it. It's scraped with small stones, and cut near the big toe joint. Where are my shoes? Can't remember if I was wearing them or not. I rub at my foot, and try to think.

Must've been running all night, but I can't remember. Last thing I remember is running out of my mother's hut. I remember my mother slapping me, and I touch my face, but that pain's all gone. Feels like a long time ago.

The memories flash back quicker now. Myrna bending over Lu. And the smell of honey.

Lu. Lying still and wizened in his cot. My heart gives a hollow thump. And goes on falling.

That's the thought that stirs me, finally. I've got to find out what happened to Lu.

Plus I'm hungry.

I get up, stiffly. Seems like I'm sore all over. And my clothes are all tattered, like they've been ripped by branches. I'll be in trouble all right – my mam'll go mad. But that's nothing that a good bowl of porridge won't fix. And mealy cakes. And stew.

Other images keep coming back to me, like flickering dreams. Someone's voice, and a humming sound. But I don't think about them because they don't make sense. Got to get home, that's all I can think about now.

I look all around, wondering which way I've come. The ground's all tangled undergrowth, and bracken and ivy. And everything's quiet, with a deep, deep quiet, like it's been silent for a thousand years. There's a tree stump, covered in ivy, looks like an old witch, hunched over. There's a jagged tree with no leaves on it, twisted and pointing. Great roots grip the earth like bony toes, and the bole of a tree that's fallen has a gaping mouth.

Too quiet, that's what it is. There's a sudden quick movement in the bushes, then a breeze passes through and it shivers and sighs, like it's breathing at me. Wish I could remember which way I've come. Haven't I always been told that the forest goes on forever? That as far as a man can walk in a day, a week, or even a month, there's only dark green forest, rolling endlessly on?

The forest swallows People, Myrna told me. *And they're never seen again.* A little girl like me'd only be a snack.

But that's daft thinking – that won't get me anywhere. I've got to set off in some direction – there's no use waiting here. I bet everyone's been out, looking for me all night. That thought makes me feel a bit better. I'll hear them shouting for me any minute, just like we did when me and Digri and the others got lost. I remember that clearly – chasing after Peglan when she ran from the story tree.

The sun's shining to one side of me, so I might as well follow it. I take a step or two then stop and pick up a stone. When I took the others to the story tree Digri cut marks in the trees with his knife. That's something we all learn, in case we go in when we shouldn't – *always leave a trail you can follow*. So now I make a jagged mark in the moss on the nearest tree with the sharp end of the stone. That's something else I've been told – that moss grows on the north side of a tree, only here it seems to be growing all round. I limp towards the next tree and make another mark. That way at least I can find my way back, and know how many paths I've tried. Or else someone'll come across the marks, and follow them and find me.

Pity I didn't think of this last night. I feel a bit sick, thinking about how I'm in the forest without a trail, and one direction looks just the same as another. My breathing sounds loud as I steady myself on the nearest tree, but I can't hear anything else, so after a moment I hobble on.

Seems like the trees are watching me make my mark, then a breath of wind stirs them and they moan and rustle. Behind me, the rest of the forest beckons, dark and trackless. But in front of me the sun shines fitfully, its long rays touching the forest floor, and I follow it, limping and hungry, only thinking of home.

Hours and hours later, when I've almost given up, the trees finally start to thin. The air changes, lighter now, and I make my way, nearly crying, towards a dazzle of leaves. I stumble on through the ivy and bracken, the trees get thinner and thinner, and suddenly there I am, at the end of the forest, blinking in the light of day.

Sun's high in the sky, and there below me are all the huts, smoke curling upwards from one of them. I hang on to the last tree and just breathe in the air, exhausted. I can hardly see for the blurring of my eyes. *Steady now, easy*, I tell myself. *You found your way in, and you were bound to find your way out again. You used your sense and followed the light. Simple.* I rub my eyes and stare down at the smoke coming from the hut. Only one fire – probably the others are all out looking for me. But there's one fire lit, and it's in my hut. *Food*, I think, and with that thought the strength comes back into my legs, and I start stumbling and tumbling down the hill.

'Mam!' I call. 'I'm back – I'm back! Mam – it's me – Keri!'

I forget everything, the pain in my side, the pain in my foot, the way she slapped me. I run down that hill, calling and crying like a great, raggedy bird. 'Mam! Mam! Mam!'

No one comes to meet me, but even that doesn't put me off. I scramble into the ditch that's round the huts and out again, then stop. And blink.

Everything seems deserted. There aren't even any pigs, or dogs. There're just two scraggy hens pecking and scratching at the bare ground by Myrna's hut.

And Myrna's not in her doorway – no one is. In fact the huts seem empty – like no one's lived in them for years.

But that's just plain daft. I pull myself together, thinking they must've taken the dogs out looking for me, and I turn towards the open doorway of my hut, ready to dart inside. I open my mouth to yell 'Mam!' again, when there's a movement inside and someone comes to the door. An old man. Someone I've never seen before.

Quick as a snake I dive into Myrna's hut. It's empty. Where is everyone? Heart banging, I peer round the open doorway. The old man's dropping a mess of vegetables on to the midden. He stops for a while, scratching. He's grey and grizzled, with a short stubble all over his face and head. He's wearing an old blue tunic with stains all over it, and grey leggings. He stares out at nothing in particular, then turns and shuffles back into the hut.

Reeling from the shock, I creep back into Myrna's hut. It's empty, like I said before, but not as though someone's just left it. Cobwebs hang from the roof, and there's an old musty smell as though no one's been in it for years. There's a broken fish trap against the wall, and a pile of rubble.

What's happening?

Something's horribly wrong.

I feel sick and dizzy from not understanding. I take

a step or two inside the hut, but suddenly my legs give way and I sink to the floor. There's a little mess of charred wood and stones where the fire used to be, a broken stool. Vividly, I remember sitting with Myrna when she told me the story about the changeling. But there's no sign of Myrna at all.

Feels like I'm dreaming. Must've fallen asleep in the forest and I'm having a bad dream. Any minute now I'll wake up.

When I don't wake up I crawl to the door again, on my hands and knees and peep round. This time there's an old woman, thin-faced and scrawny, sitting at the doorway of the hut, shelling peas.

My hut! I think, and through all the sickness and fear I feel a pang of anger. I should go up to her and ask her what's going on. But my heart's banging and thudding, and there's a watery feeling in my stomach, like I might be sick. All I can think is – *we've been attacked in the night, and strangers have come and taken over our huts.* Like when the raiders came, and killed my father.

But that thought's too big, too awful. My chest hurts just thinking about it. And anyway, there's no one else here. I peer round at the other huts. Everywhere's got the same deserted feel. Doorways hanging open; roofs part fallen in. But no sign of warriors; no sign of a fight. Just two old people, and two scraggy hens, and the empty, broken-down huts.

How could all that have happened, in just one night?

Then another thought comes to me. I must've left the forest at the wrong place, and come on another settlement, just like mine. Same number of huts, same ditch, only halfway finished, different people.

A wave of relief floods through me, though I'm still scared. That has to be it. I always knew we couldn't be the only settlers in the forest.

I'll have to get myself back into the forest somehow without being seen, and start again. When the old woman gets up and goes back indoors, I creep away from the hut.

It's then that I see it – Digri's charm, still swinging in the doorway of his hut. Dried heather and bird bones and feathers, to keep the faeries away. It's hanging to one side, and half of the feathers have gone and there's no heather left, but I recognize it straight away, and a sour bile rises in my throat.

And just then the old man comes out once again. He's carrying another bowl, and walking straight towards me. I stand stock still, staring, but he doesn't even see me. And that's when I realize – he's like Myrna, near enough blind.

He's about to walk right past me when I step forward and grab the bowl. Don't know what I'm thinking – I just want to ask him: *What's happening? What's going on? And where's my mother?* But he gives a short yell and drops the bowl. Water and vegetable peelings gush all over my feet. He clutches something at his throat and shouts for all he's worth.

'Wife!' he yells. 'Wife!'

And the scrawny woman darts out of the hut, with a pot in one hand and a long knife in the other.

No time to think. I'm running, fast as a hare, scrambling back up the hill to the forest.

Nobody's following.

Slowly, my heart stops banging in my ears, and my breathing slows down. That old couple couldn't catch a lame hen.

Even so, I crawl under the cover of a hawthorn bush and crouch there, sick and shaken.

I can't think what to do.

I just can't think.

None of it makes sense.

I bury my face in my hands and wait for my thoughts to make sense. There're two of them, mainly.

One is, I've come out of the forest at the wrong place, different from where I went in. I lift my head up and look around to check.

But there's Mabb's Hill with the bump on top and the little bit scooped out of the side, as though someone's dipped into it with a spoon. And there's the boulder, like an old man, turned into stone. And somewhere below me I can hear the river burbling on, the same that Lu fell in, where me and Digri and the others built a dam, and chased the Peggotty Witch.

Digri, I think, and my heart breaks into mourning. What wouldn't I give to have him walk up to me now, round-faced and whistling, and tell me it's all been a joke.

When that doesn't happen, I stare mournfully down at the settlement. It's our settlement all right – it's where I live.

Maybe the raiders have been.

This second thought comes to me with a sickening thump. Raiders have been, killed everyone, or took them away, and left two old people in their place.

But the two old people look like they've always been there – like they were just making breakfast.

And why does everything looks so deserted, and broken down? How can all that have happened in just one night?

I spread out my hands and my fingers are shaking. Something else is pressing on me – something I don't even want to know.

I stare all around, as though looking for clues, and that's when it comes to me, the thought I didn't want to have.

All the birds are singing and calling. One lands in the tree next to me and pecks at the blossom.

May blossom.

There's a straggle of bluebells that've lately been in flower under the next tree. Wood sorrel, and anemones. The thrush next to me sings so sharply it hurts my head and I start to shiver and shake. I hug myself to stop the shaking from spreading, and next thing I know I'm retching and all the bile and water in my stomach comes flooding up through my mouth and nose.

I'm sick till I can't be sick any more, and I crawl away from my own vomit and lie on the ground, panting like a wild animal. And when I open my eyes I see the petals of the wood sorrel, like pale stars, in front of me.

It's spring. Late spring, early summer. Only when I ran away from my hut, and my mother, and Lu, it was autumn.

Well, I can't lie here forever. Even though my whole body's hurting, and the world doesn't make sense. Somehow I've fallen asleep and slept right through the winter, like a bear, and now I've woken up and everything's changed. But I can't live here, in the forest – I don't know how. I've come up with a plan. Not a very good plan, but the best I can do.

I have to go back to the huts and try to talk to

someone there – to tell them I'm lost and find out what I can. Then, if they chase me away again, all I can do is try to make my way round the edge of the forest – not *through* it because that way I might never be seen again, but round the edges – looking for everyone, my mother, and Digri and Myrna and Bryn and Lu. And I'll go on looking, finding what I can to eat, until something kills me or I drop down dead – even if it takes a hundred years.

I have a funny feeling when I think this, as though I might cry, but I shake it off. *Don't talk daft*, I tell myself. *It didn't take a hundred years to get here, did it?* And my mother wouldn't just leave me – she'll be out somewhere, looking. And cupping this thought in my mind like a candle flame, I get up slowly and set off once more down the hill.

A bit of sackcloth hangs loosely from one window and flaps in the breeze. It's even plainer to me now that the only hut still occupied is the one I used to live in, that's got the old man in it now, and his shrew-like wife. I creep towards it, and see the light from a fire flickering through the window. The door's shut. Probably locked. I should knock at it, but instead I press myself up to the wall near the window, listening.

'You didn't see anything then?' comes the old woman's voice, thin and rasping, and the old man just mumbles a reply.

'Could've been a goblin. Or a sprite.'

The old man mumbles again, and she lays into him.

'Speak up, can't you? You know I can't tell what you're saying when you mumble on!'

'I've told you before,' the old man says. 'I couldn't see it proper – light were in my eyes.'

'You can't see at all,' the old woman says scornfully. 'I keep telling you – you're near enough blind.'

'And you're deaf,' the old man mutters.

'What did you say?'

'Never mind.'

'Well – whatever it is – it'll have to be found,' says the old woman. 'We can't live with it here – boggart-spooked. What did you say it looked like again?'

The old man sighs. 'I told you – I couldn't see it clearly. But what I saw were like green and grey tatters in the wind – like some wild forest thing.'

I look down at myself. It's true that my clothes are all in tatters. And greenish-grey. Like someone's caught up a pile of leaves from the forest floor and sewn them together. Badly.

'Well, whatever it is, it'll have to be found,' says the old woman sharply. 'If you were man enough you'd be out there now, hunting it down.'

'Nay, not I,' says the old man fearfully. 'I'm not going out there hunting some wick thing, that'll lead me on to the Lost Paths, or change me into some fey beast. We've had enough ill luck as it is!'

Then the old woman gives him the sharp edge of her tongue, shrew that she is, and I can't help but smile. So that's what they think I am – something fey, or wick, a boggart or a goblin. It's then that I come up with my great plan.

I'm starving, of course. For all I know, I've not eaten all winter. Plus I've been sick. And there's a great pan of pottage on the fire. If I just knock at the door and try to talk to them, chances are they'll drive me away. Especially if they think I'm from Faerie. Seems to me they're a bit simple-minded. They might not even be able to answer my questions. So my plan is food first; questions later.

I stand to one side of the window and call in through it, making my voice high and keening, like the wind through the reeds.

'Old man!' I call softly. 'Old ma-an!'

Even though I can't see them, I can hear the old man clutching his wife.

'What was that!' he hisses, spluttering food.

'What was what?' says the old woman, shaking him off. 'I didn't hear anything!'

She must be really deaf, I think, and try again, cupping my hands round my mouth.

'Old ma-an – come to me. Don't be afraid – I'm calling you!'

I'm really good at this – didn't know I could make my voice sound so eerie. The old man's nearly bursting his britches. 'There – there!' he cries in a sobbing moan, and 'Where – where?' cries his wife.

What a pair! Him nearly blind and her nearly deaf. Don't know how they've stayed alive so long. I don't feel sorry for them, though. They're in *my* hut.

'Come to me now!' I cry, in a mournful, hooting tone. Next minute, the door's bursting open and the old woman runs out with a stick.

'Come and get me – boggart!' she yells, brandishing it like a demon.

This is my chance. I seize a scatter of pebbles and throw them as far as I can. One bounds off the wall of Myrna's hut and the old woman runs after it, distracted, and waving her stick. I whip round and in through the doorway, into the dim hut.

I'd considered leaping out at the old man and yelling *Boo!* But he's not even looking. He's huddled in a corner, weeping and covering his eyes with his blanket. Meanwhile, on the table, there's a great steaming bowl of stew, so I grab it and run out of the door again, whipping round the corner just as the old woman returns, her stick lowered, looking confused. She goes back into her hut, and I grin at the squawk she makes when she sees that the food's all gone. I can hear her setting about her husband with the stick, but I don't wait to hear more. I hurry to the old storehouse and crouch down, wolfing all the food down at once, then finish with a happy belch.

This is a good game and I've not finished yet. I lick the bowl clean, I'm that hungry, and put it to one side for future use. When I look out again, the old man's pinning a piece of bread to the doorway with a peg. I laugh at this – a short, snickering laugh. I know what he's up to – stale bread's supposed to keep faeries out. And there's the old woman, scattering rowan leaves and herbs and daisies all round the hut. The old man looks around fearfully, this way then that, then runs away from the hut in a shuffling, stumbling run, and comes back with the hens, flapping and squawking under each arm. They take the hens in with them, obviously afraid that the boggart, or me, will kill and eat them if they leave them outside. Then I can hear them shutting and bolting the door, and dragging things across it to make it safe.

All this to keep me out – me!

When they've quite finished, I sneak up to the door and grab the bread off its peg and cram it into my mouth. Strangely enough, it tastes funny, and crumbles like soil in my mouth. And I don't like the smell of the herbs, so sharp and bitter in my nose that they make my eyes sting. But I tell myself it's only like one of Myrna's evil brews, and I rattle the door viciously to show them I could get in if I wanted to, and I howl and whine at the shutter at the window and throw stones at it, and run round the house widder-ways shrieking just like a real boggart. Giving them something to be feared of.

I only stop when I'm out of breath and exhausted. Then I peep in through one of the cracks in the shutters.

I can just about see them, clutching one another. The old man's shaking like a leaf in the wind, and the woman's as grey as death. I fling another scattering of stones at the shutters, then hobble over to the old storehouse again. Think I'll have a proper look round it, just in case there's some food there I might have missed.

In fact, I do find an old turnip, but it looks a bit off-putting – wormy and half-eaten already, and the surface like wood. I eat it anyway, and search for more.

There's a sack in the corner that might be useful to sleep on, except when I shake it it's full of beetles and dust. A hatch in the floor leads down to the underground hide, and a stink rises as I lift it. I crawl into it now, half fearing what I might find. This is where we hid when the raiders came. There's a quick, flittering movement, and my heart gives a sickening leap, but it's only a mouse. What did I think it would be? Ghosts? A dead body, groping towards the light?

I crawl all the way in, and the smell's mouldy and damp, but there's nothing else. Nobody I know is crouching there, hiding, waiting to jump out at me. There's only the memory of the night my father died, run through with spears.

There's nothing I can do about that memory, nothing at all. So I grit my teeth and crawl out again.

Light's fading now. I don't want to go back to the forest. I've got to sleep somewhere, but I don't want to sleep on my own. I want to be near people, however unfriendly they are. And the old man and the old woman have shut me out for the night. So I might as well stay here – in this dank, damp smelly place.

I shake out the sacking once again, disturbing yet more beetles and ants, and crawl in under it, holding my breath.

When I close my eyes I can see my mother's face, smiling the way she smiled at harvest time. I can see Digri and Peglan and Ogda and Arun. And Bryn. And Lu.

I can't help it, I start to sniff. A great tear rolls from my eye, hurting a little as it squeezes out. It falls to the earth floor, and lies there like a little jewelled stone.

I'm so surprised by this I stop crying. I pick it up. It's a little stone – tear-shaped and twinkling in my hand. I've seen ones like this before. Sometimes me and Digri would find them, by the river, and run to show someone – my mother, or Digri's dad. Elf stones, they called them.

I stare at it, baffled, then try to squeeze out another. But it's no use – I can't cry to order. And I'm too tired to think about it much. I put it away in my mind, together with all the other things I don't understand about today. There's a lot of them in there. Soon there'll hardly be room for anything else.

I shift and turn about on the sacking. Ground's bumpy and hard and I can't get comfortable. I try bending my arms and legs into different positions. Then I fold myself up, right up and tucked over smaller and smaller, till I'm taking up hardly any room at all, like a nut in its shell. Never tried that before. But once I'm as folded over as I can get, I fall asleep straight away – I can even hear myself snoring. And that does strike me as strange, but no stranger than anything else that's happened to me this day.

Sleep's strange, as well. Full of flickering shadows and coloured lights. And great cobwebby rooms, with a voice like music saying slowly, 'I do wish you'd help me –'. But before I can hear what I have to do I pull myself awake, with a real wrench, as though the dream's sucking me under, just like the river tried to once. And I can hardly credit it, but it's daylight already. Light pours in through the open doorway, so strong and yellow it makes me wince and curl up again on my sacking. But then this small, fierce hope flares in me – that everything that happened to me yesterday might have been a dream, so I get up quickly and hurry outside to look.

Nothing. Everything's just as it was – deserted, broken-down huts, weeds growing tall, planks of wood and rubble strewn all over. Disappointment stabs me so hard I want to shout and yell, then I feel a wave of sickness and I just stand there, like a wilting weed. Trying to take it all in, trying to believe it – I'm stuck here, in this place where I don't want to be, and everything I once knew and loved has gone. Too much, too much. It's swelling up in my head like a seed pod about to burst.

Then I turn my darkest gaze on to the hut where the little old man and the little old woman have shut themselves in. My hut.

I creep towards it quietly. Notice something at the door. They've left food out for me – just like Myrna used to for the faeries, to keep them quiet. A few miserable grains of barley and some squashed-looking berries. Call that food? It'll take more than that to keep me quiet.

I cram it all down anyway. Because I'm starving. Seems like I'm always hungry now. I stand by the window, cramming every last crumb into my mouth. Then I hear a stirring inside. I peep through the crack in the shutter.

The old man's sitting on the side of the bed in a greyish shirt that falls below his knees. His two feet are planted flat on the floor, squarish, the veins in them knotted like boles on a tree trunk, the nails curved and yellow and horny. The old woman's hunched over a pot on the fire.

'Stew's nearly boiled down,' she says. 'We'll need water.'

The old man says nothing to this. He scratches himself, rubs his bleary eyes. Then he says, 'I dreamed I had a sister last night.'

The old woman doesn't even look up. 'You did have a sister,' she says sourly. 'And I had a brother.'

'No – but I dreamed she was here,' the old man says. 'Living with us. Only she was no more than a child. The same age mine would have been when she –'

'There's no use talking like that,' snaps the old woman. 'That's all past and gone. We've both had people we've loved and lost. Only difference is you weren't old enough to remember yours. But I remember mine – do you think I don't? Not a day goes past but I don't think of them –'

Her voice rises as though she might cry, and he interrupts her then.

'Nay, now – don't upset yourself,' he says soothingly. 'It was only a dream. I'm allowed to dream, aren't I?'

The old woman says nothing to this. Then she says, 'One of them hens'll have to go in the pot. You'll have to fetch water. And I need to check the barn for eggs.'

I've heard enough. They'll have to go out sooner or later, and then I'll see what mischief I can make. I skulk round the side of the hut, waiting.

Don't have to wait long. The old woman comes to the door. She's nervous enough, looking this way and that, but then she sets off at a scurry to the hen house, bent over but nimble, and returns carrying two or three eggs in a cloth. A little while passes, then the man comes to the door, carrying a pot. He sets off in his hobbling way, looking neither to right nor left. Takes a bit longer, but soon he's hobbling back, carrying water that sloshes and splashes a little.

Can't help but wonder how blind he is. He gets closer and closer, then, greatly daring, I step away from the wall right in front of him.

He doesn't even blink. I have to leap back quick or he'd walk right into me. But he does pass a hand quickly in front of his eyes before he goes in, as though he might've seen something funny from the corner of one of them. Makes me feel strange, that. As though I might really not be there at all.

I don't think about that for long. I've realized now how much trouble I can make. The rest of that morning they get bolder about leaving the hut, not even checking to see whether the boggart's about.

Then my chance comes, when they both leave. I slip into the hut.

I have a fine old time then, chasing the hens about and tipping over the broth. The hens flap and squawk, dropping their dirt and feathers everywhere. I smash two of the eggs against the wall and eat the third. Then I break what pots I can find and rip up a sheet the old woman's been mending, and spill all the water on to the floor.

The old woman comes running, hearing the hens, and I flatten myself against the wall. She stops dead in the doorway with her mouth as far open as it'll go, so I can't help but chuckle.

She closes her mouth and opens it again. Air rushes out of her and she sucks it back in. Then it happens. She screams out for all she's worth.

'Lu!' she screams. 'Lu!'

There's a noise like a high wind howling through my head. The whole world turns itself over then shakes itself down.

'Lu!' she squawks again, and the old man comes running.

'What is it?' he cries. 'What's happening?'

But he isn't Lu – he can't be called Lu, I'm thinking, over and over.

His eyes are wide open, though of course he can't see. I can see, though. I'm looking right into his eyes. And they're greenish, and filmy now, but there's a brown speckle in the left one.

No, no, no, no, no, no, no!

'Boggarts've been in – boggarts –' the old woman's gabbling. 'The hens – and the eggs – and the stew!'

The old man can't see the mess. He gropes for his wife's arm. And the next words he says send my stomach tumbling over and my world crashing to the floor like the stew.

'Settle down, Ogda,' he says. 'What is it that's happened?'

Then all the horror and protest I feel comes bursting out of my mouth. 'NOOOOOOOOOOOOOO!' I howl.

The old man and the old woman clutch one another in dismay, but they're looking at each other, not at me. 'Did you hear that?' the old woman says, and the old man tries to calm her, though he's shaken up himself.

'It were only the wind, creaking the gate,' he says.

I can't stand this any more.

'Only the –? Hear this, you great lug-eared lump!' I cry, and I step out right in front of them.

But neither of them even looks up. The old man guides the old woman over to their bed in the corner, and she sits on it, shaking. 'Oh, Lu – everything's smashed and broken – and there was no one in the house. It wasn't you, and it wasn't me –'

'It was me – me!' I shriek, dancing about in front of them, but the old woman only wipes her eyes. 'Whatever's happening to us, Lu? We're boggart-spooked for sure.'

'Stop calling him Lu!' I yell, right in front of them, then I have an idea. I rattle all the remaining pots, and jiggle the table about and pick up the stool and hurl it at the wall. The old man looks terrified, scrambling backwards on the bed and still holding on to his wife. And she just covers her face with her apron and cries.

Then I notice something else. A cord round his neck. My stomach lurches horribly, and I stride straight towards them. It's so strange to see him looking straight through me with Lu's eyes, wide and terrified and unseeing. I put out my hand and grab the cord. He gives a short yell as I yank it away from his shirt. Then I look at it, and what's left of my world comes tumbling down.

It's my amulet. The one my father carved for me. The one I gave to Lu.

I sink down then, with a groan that seems to come up through me, right from the middle of the earth. I crumple up on the floor and cover my face with my hands, and for a short while there is only silence.

After a while they start whispering to one another in low, worried voices.

'Has it gone yet?'

'Well – it's gone quiet.'

'Might be waiting for us to move.'

'It grabbed me, round my neck.'

'What was it?' And so on.

I'm hardly listening, grappling with the thought that these two old people might be Little Ogda and Lu.

How long can I have been in the forest?

Nothing makes sense any more. I still feel as though I'm in some dark, terrible dream. But if I am, it's going on longer than any dream I've ever had. And I can't seem to wake up. I lift my head wearily, and look round at the smashed and broken hut.

'Is everything broken?' the old man says.

'Everything,' says the old woman. 'We've lost everything.'

'What've we done to deserve this?' says the old man, raising his voice now, though the old woman shushes him. 'Have we not had misfortune enough?'

Then they have a short discussion, about whether they should get up and look around to see if I've really gone, but neither of them moves. I've scared them both to death, I think, and for the first time I feel ashamed.

'If only we could've had children,' the old woman says wearily. 'A fine son, to help us with the work of

106

the farm. Or a daughter to look after us in our old age.'

Where is everyone? I think suddenly. Why are these two left here on their own? What happened to everyone else? To Digri and Peglan, and Arun? What happened to Tilse's baby? Or to Tilse, for that matter.

'Whoever would've thought there'd only be the two of us left, out of all our People?' the old woman says. 'Oh, Lu, Lu – whatever'll become of us?'

The old man tries to comfort her then. 'Nay, Ogda, Ogda, don't take on so,' he says. But I've heard enough. Shame wells up in me like a big dark pool, and tears press like little stones at the back of my eyes. *I should help them*, I think suddenly. *I should help them to clear everything up and start again.* But that would only scare them even more.

I slink over to the door and lift the latch, glancing back briefly to the bed, where they're still holding on to one another. Just for a moment I see them as they were when I left. Little Ogda with her two short plaits and her runny nose; my brother Lu, with his round face and sunny smile. It's like looking at the sweet kernel of a withered old nut. But I can't ask them what's happened – they won't even hear me.

Neither of them looks in my direction. I open the door just a chink, and slip outside, closing it gently behind me.

In the bright light the huts look even more deserted than before. The hens are pecking and scrabbling about again on the hard ground. There's a fluttering movement in the corner of my eye. Digri's charm, stirring in the breeze.

Somehow, the sight of that brings home the full horror of where I am. I can't stand it any more – I can't look at these deserted huts where everyone I once knew used to live and play. I set off, walking away from them, not even knowing where I'm going, just that I've got to get away. Faster and faster I go, away from the huts, away from the forest, picking up speed till I'm skimming over the earth and stones and grass, running downhill towards the river.

It's in the river that I first catch sight of myself. I scramble on to a large stone and lie there, face downwards and gasping for breath. Thoughts are whirling in my head like thistlefluff in the wind, and I can't grasp hold of any of them.

The water's calm and clear, I can see little fish swimming about near the bottom like brown shadows. I can see the shadow of my head, hair sticking out all over like a bird's nest. Then the sun shifts, or something happens, and for a moment I see myself clearly – a little fey, wick thing, greenish in the water, grinning up at me with glittery eyes. I only catch a glimpse of it before the water breaks everything up, but I start back in fear. It doesn't look like me – not like any me I recognize, and I glance back in case anyone or anything's looking over my shoulder. But nothing is, of course. Cautiously, I peer back again.

There it is again, with its little pointy features and horrible urchin grin.

I'm not grinning but my reflection is.

I scramble back and look at my hands. Nut brown, with pointy fingers. I stare at them like I've never seen them before.

My toes are the same – thin and pointy.

Not human.

Terrified, I peek in the water again. There it is – the wild hair all tangled in leaves and twigs, the greeny-brown face and strange, glittering eyes.

Only this time it's taking no notice of me at all. It's eating an apple.

And I feel sick – sick to my stomach.

'Boggart-spooked' that old couple said they were. They called me boggart. And they couldn't see or hear me.

I look again at my tattered clothes. They're greyish-green, like the old man said, as if I'm stuck all over with leaves.

I open my mouth and yell at it. It's a yell like nothing I've ever heard before. It whips up the water and spins it round. When I can see my reflection again, it's got its mouth open too, but it isn't yelling. Just looking at me like it's wondering what all the fuss is about. I stamp in the water, breaking the image up, and it shakes its fist back at me. And that's when I start to run.

I run and run away from the water. Back up the hill, shouting and waving my arms about like a lunatic. Then I stop, panting for breath.

Before me are the huts, where the old man and the old woman are. Can't go back there.

Beyond that's the forest. Can't go back there.

There's nowhere to go. Nowhere at all.

Don't want to go back to the river either. But I do want to see my reflection one more time. Hoping and hoping that I'll see myself the way I used to be. Steps dragging, I make my way back.

But there I am again, a little pointy goblin, or elf, or – well, I don't know what I am any more.

I keep on peering back into the water, willing myself to change into something I recognize, but however often I look, the reflection's the same. Or not the same – sometimes it's looking away from me, sometimes sideways on, like it's doing its own thing. But it's still got the same pointy features, and bird's nest hair, and horrid grin. Somewhere in it I can still recognize the girl I used to be, but something's changed me. I feel all over my face with my hands but that doesn't tell me much. I go on looking at this reflection that seems to have a life of its own, until I get tired, and fling myself backwards on the stone, staring upwards into the high blue sky.

Nothing seems real.

Nothing's right.

Feels like nothing'll ever be right again.

Why aren't I old, like Ogda and Lu?

Something happened to me in the forest – that's for sure. Something got hold of me and changed me.

But how? And why?

And that's as far as I get. Because, try as I might, I can't remember a single thing about the night I spent in the forest. Nothing between running in and coming out again. My head starts spinning when I try to think of it, or it fills up with mist, like a cloud rolling over a hill. But until I know that, I'll never know what's happened to my mother, and Bryn, and Myrna, and Digri, and Peglan and Derry, and Arun and Griff and Tilse, Arval and Mabda and Gwern.

And naming them all like this in my mind makes the pain come. Swelling and bursting in my chest.

If they're all gone, really and forever gone, I can't take it. My heart'll crack like a hatching egg.

Then the pain comes bursting out of my mouth, in a great howling cry. But the sound I make isn't human at all – it's a great jumble of noises. Like wind and rain thrashing the bushes, branches creaking, wolves howling and the high lonely call of a bird. And it goes on and on, longer than I knew I had breath, until finally I shut my mouth and the noise stops, and I fall back on to the stone and shut my eyes.

I must've fallen asleep because the next thing I know, I'm opening my eyes, and the light's fading. The first faint stars are overhead, and through the babbling of the river I can hear a woman's voice singing, sweet and low.

It's the most beautiful singing I've ever heard – like leaves in a summer breeze or the wind rippling through grass. Seems like it's calling the stars out because while I lie there, enchanted, more of them appear, deeper and brighter in the sky. And the whole world's hushed, listening, the willows bent over the water and the reeds moving to the sound of the song. For there're words in it, but when I try to remember them, they don't make any sense. Something like this:

> *Neither sleep, neither lie*
> *Years like leaves go fluttering by*
> *Years like bones on the forest floor*
> *Summer rain on an autumn door . . .*

Seems like nonsense, but at the same time it makes perfect sense. And I get up, as though in a dream, and follow the singing:

> *Has the goose gone to its nest?*
> *Has the fox gone to its rest?*
> *Only the forest knows . . .*

I'm wading through the river, and I can't even feel the cold. I follow the bank round a curve, and the music seems now near, now far away. But while I listen to it I seem to forget everything, all my hurts and problems. I forget what I look like in the water, or that no one can see or hear me any more, and even that I've lost everyone I love. All I can do is follow the low sweet sound of that music, round one curve of the river, then another. And there, in the dusk, in the fading light, I see her. All wrapped in grey, and dipping her cloth into the water. The Peggotty Witch.

The Peggotty Witch? Making that sweet music? Never knew she could sing. I heard that she could only make animal noises, like grunts and brayings and droning. But here she is, singing sweeter than the sweetest bird, so that all the fish swim to the surface, listening.

I start to wade through the water, when suddenly I remember what's said about her. If you get right up to her without her seeing you, and catch hold of her washing, she's got to answer three questions. So I duck down low and creep out of the water and along the bank.

Didn't know I could move so fast or so quiet. Closer and closer I get to the little shrouded figure, and as I creep towards her, her song changes:

> There was an old woman
> And her name was Peg,
> And her head was of wood
> And she had a cork leg.
> Pitch her, pitch her into the water
> She'll tell you no lie
> She's the river's daughter.

Then, when I get right up to her, still creeping like a snake, she says:

> Pixie in the moonlight
> Pixie in the dew,
> Fly away, pixie
> Where the wind never blew.

So now she knows I'm here. I'm scuppered then. Can't ask her my questions. I'm so disappointed, I almost turn away.

On the other hand, here's this witchety old woman

I never even knew could talk before. She might've seen something, or heard what's happened to me. So I slide down the bank towards her and stand at her side, but not so close that she can reach me with her washing.

She doesn't turn round, just keeps washing the clothes. After a minute I say, 'So much washing, old woman – where'd you get all these clothes from?'

It's not what I meant to say, and not very polite. But she only shoots me a look, sly-like, and says, 'One.'

'One what?' I ask her.

'Two,' she says.

I look at her, baffled, but she just goes on pulling out more washing from beneath her shawl. 'How is it you can talk?' I ask her. 'I heard you can only grunt or squeak.'

'That's the third,' she says, pulling out yet more washing. And suddenly I know what she's talking about. I've asked her three questions – only none of them were the questions I meant to ask.

I feel a stab of rage then. Curse myself for being stupid. Feel like pushing her into the river, but all I say is, 'Well – you haven't answered any.'

She turns to me then, and I feel a pang of fear when I see her face. One nostril in her broad squat nose, a single tooth in her mouth and glassy, milk-pale eyes. I look down, away from her face, and there are her red, webbed feet, but all she says, mildly, is, 'Give us a hand for washing with.'

'Why should I?' I say, even more rudely than before, but she only cackles and dumps a bundle of washing at my feet.

'Questions, questions, questions,' she says, shifting about on her funny feet. 'More questions than washing. Can you wash them clothes – that's my question.'

I glare at her, then look down at the clothes. Doesn't look like much. 'What if I do?' I ask her. 'Will you answer my questions then?'

She rolls her lidless eyes. 'Questions, questions all the time,' she says to herself. 'Don't do questions, do washing. Got to do the washing before the moon's up full.'

I glance up at the moon. The rim of it's just appearing over the ridge of Mabb's Hill. Well – I haven't got anything better to do. Haven't got anything to do at all. And if I help her, maybe she'll help me. I bend down and pick up the first item from the bundle.

It's a woman's smock, all covered in stains of one sort or another – meat and berries – I can hardly make them out in the dusk. I turn it this way and that, and even sniff at it, not sure what to do. But finally I copy her and hold it in the water.

Instantly, all the stains stream away from it. I laugh in astonishment. Never knew washing was this easy – we never did much of it at home. I try to hand it back to the Peggotty Witch, but she shakes her head.

'Let it go,' she says, letting her own garment flow and billow away in the water.

I do as I'm told, and the smock billows out for a moment in the stream, just as if there's someone inside it, then it turns round slowly and drifts away. I have a funny feeling, like I ought to remember what the washing is. Feels creepy, and at the same time the most natural thing in the world. Like I've always been doing it.

'There's another,' she says, handing me a piece of dirty grey linen that looks as though a baby might've been wrapped in it. I hold it in the water again, and all the dirt streams away from it so it's snowy white. Then I let it go, and once again it billows out, then takes on a baby's shape before it folds and turns and drifts away.

It reminds me of something I don't want to remember, so I hold my tongue and dip the next piece in, and the next. Bundle's bigger than it looks. Just when I think I've come to the end of it, there's another piece in the tied-up cloth.

'Why do you do so much washing?' I say at last, pulling out yet another piece. I've forgotten she doesn't answer questions, but this time she says, 'Washing, washing's all there is.' Then she adds, 'Terrible dirty folk, humans.'

Well, it's not really an answer, but it's the only one I'm likely to get. And there's no time for talking because there's so much washing, and the moon's rising steadily over that hill. So I carry on, dipping each piece in the water and letting it float away. Can't help wondering if it'll ever find its owners again. And if it doesn't, then what's the point?

She carries on washing too, bending and dipping in the water, humming and muttering to herself:

> *Wash-a-day, wash-a-day,*
> *Wash the stains and dirt away.*
> *When it's done, begin again,*
> *That's the way to live with men.*

'Great,' I mutter, but she doesn't hear. Or she acts like she doesn't. She just goes on washing and the moon goes on rising, and, finally, when my arms are aching and my back too, she says, 'Done!' and lays the final pieces out on the bank to dry.

This is it. The moment I've been waiting for, to ask my question.

Funny thing is, I can't speak. My tongue's gone funny, and I can't think clearly what I need to ask. My heart starts hammering and my stomach twists, in case I get it all wrong and I lose her without having a chance to ask the right thing, the thing I need to know.

Then she turns to me, and too late I see the demon light in her eyes. The moon's full overhead, and the reflection of it glows red in each lidless eye. She raises a finger and points at me and says:

> *In the forest, in the forest*
> *Forty years and more.*
> *You want to go back, go back,*
> *But you cannot find the door.*
> *Time to remember*
> *What you did before.*

I stare at her, speechless. *Forty years and more?* But she's unwinding a cloth from her shawl. It's all stained and dirty. She says something like, 'This is the sheet of your memory. You need to wash it clean.'

She throws it towards me and I catch one end. Then she starts to fold and crumple, so there's nothing left of her but a bundle of clothes, like she's turned into old washing herself. I look around wildly, but I can't see her. Just the bole of a tree and branches swaying, and the river burbling on.

I look down at the sheet in my hands. One more thing to wash. I jerk it impatiently into the river. What else is there to do? I keep hold of one end and let the river tug and pull at the rest of it. And just like before, the stains start to flow away.

The sheet billows out in the stream, twisting and

turning. It unfolds slowly, into the shape of something I recognize, then folds again. But the river's straightening it out, almost flat, and I can see it all spread out before me. *Like bedding*, I think. It's even bunched up at one end into a shape like a pillow. It is a bed, I can see that now, and it's a bed I've seen before.

Even as I think this thought, I hear the voice. The same voice that came to me in my dreams.

'I do wish you'd help me,' it says, 'to make my bed.'

That's when I start to remember. Memories float like thistledown through my mind, whirling faster and faster. I'm in a swirling storm of thistledown, flying all around me like flakes of snow. And that voice, sweet and pure, like honey in my ear.

'Do help me,' it says.

Then it's as though I'm watching myself in a dream. Everything's happening really slowly. We gather the bones of little wild animals, crickets and shrews, and link them all together into a kind of bedstead – that was the word she used for it – not hard and rigid like the ground, but springy.

The *bedhead* is made from snail shells. We only gather the ones where the snail has already been pecked out by birds, and we lift up the silvery trail that the snail leaves and use it to fasten the shells together, and we smear it over them too, like a gloss, so that it shimmers in the moonlight. It takes a long time, but not as long as the mattress, and the pillow and coverlet, which are made from thistledown and woven together with spiders' webs. Then the final coverlet was made from insects' wings, drawn together with more cobweb thread.

Doesn't it hurt them? I asked.

Oh, no, said the voice, so sweet, and wise and kind. *They love company. And to be brought together in beauty – all things love that.*

And the coverlet was beautiful. Made from the wings of damselflies, mayflies, dragonflies, butterflies and moths, all held together by a shimmering silken thread. It hovered just above the bed, droning softly, in a gentle lullaby.

Feel it, she murmured, and it brushed against my skin like a fabric of woven dreams. To lie on that bed would be like lying on air, wrapped in a cloud while the sweet humming lulled you gently to sleep.

But we hadn't finished yet. We had to gather more cobwebs for curtains and droplets of water from the spiders' webs we'd collected and hang them around the room for starlight to shine through, like lamps.

Then at last the bed was done, shell-shaped and glimmering, and she lay down on it with a sigh of contentment and bliss.

And I stood over her, bent almost double, clutching

a stick for support with my wrinkled, withered old hands.

Can I go now? I asked.

Go? she responded, sitting up again, her hair like a fall of water on to the bed. *I had hoped that for my sake you would stay.*

But even in my dream-like state I knew I wanted to get home. I had spent too much time – so much time – with this beautiful stranger, and now I had to get back. *My mother would be worried*, I said, in my thick, rasping voice that could not have contrasted more with her musical tones.

She laughed a little when I said this, then sighed a sigh of gentle regret.

It is a perfect bed, she said. *There is none better. Since you have done your job so well, I will give you a gift. And that gift will be . . .*

She traced a pattern on the coverlet with her finger – I can still see the pearly fingernail.

. . . you will not return to your people old and frail as you are now, but young, and healthy, and full of life as you were when I found you. That way I hope that one day you may return. But you must leave me something in exchange . . .

With one part of my mind I can hear myself groaning aloud as I remember all this. Because now I can see the strangeness of it all, the weird enchantment I had fallen into, though at the time it made perfect sense.

Slowly the white thistledown stops whirling around me. I'm on the bank of the river once more, still holding the sheet that billows and tosses in the water. I let it go and it folds and turns and drifts away. But I've seen all I want to see. I drop to my knees on the muddy bank, horror and despair welling up in me. I'm in no doubt at all about who the beautiful stranger is.

Mabb.

Mabb, Mabb, Mabb! Queen of the Faeries. The wicked enchantress who steals men's lives away.

And she's stolen mine!

I can remember more now, though it all feels like a dream. I remember finding her in the forest, or at least, coming to a little round hut in a clearing. There was light pouring from it, and it seemed like the most welcoming place in the world. And I was so tired and hungry that I went inside. Then everything's blurred, but she must've taken me in and fed me. And made me work for her. For more than forty years! And all because . . .

Because she wanted me to make her bed!

This thought is so huge and horrible, I can hardly bear to think it.

But I can't not think it. It comes bursting and

burning up into my mind, until I can't think anything else. She left my brother and took me, just like I asked her to. But while I was away, everything changed. Everyone I knew and loved grew old and died, or just grew old, without me. She tricked me into coming back to a world where everything I knew had gone!

The full horror of what's happened comes to me, and I open my mouth to let it out in a howl of rage.

MAAAABB!!!!

All the rage and pain and sorrow of the world comes bursting out of me in that one desperate howl. And when I finish I'm empty, weak and shaking. I could roll into the river myself and let myself drift away.

But not yet. Not yet. I haven't finished yet. It isn't over.

What did she say to me? *In the hope that you might return?*

Well, I'll return all right. I'll give her something to think about. I'll take her life the way that she's taken mine.

Except that I don't know how.

What was it in Myrna's story – something about the gates of the wind and the door of the rain?

What's that supposed to mean?

The woman in the story didn't know either, though. She just had to set off.

Slowly, I lift my face up and look around. My heart's beating thick and fast. But nothing else has changed. I'm on the bank of the river, alone. The Peggotty Witch has gone and the night's drawing on. One thing I know for certain is that I don't want to go back to the huts where my little brother's turned into an old, old man, who can't see or hear me, and where Little Ogda looks older than Myrna.

But where else can I go, what else can I do?

Suddenly I see the bundle of clothing that is all that's left of the Peggotty Witch. I go over to it and shake it, thinking perhaps that I'll shake her back into them. It's a complete set of clothes, cloak and tunic, leggings, cloak. And shoes, though I'm fairly sure she wasn't wearing shoes before. And they look as though they'd be my size.

I glance down at myself, suddenly conscious of the naked flesh peeping through my tattered rags.

Well, what else is there to do? I put them on. I strip off my rags and let them drift away in the water, and pull on the tunic, cloak, leggings and little pointed shoes. All greenish, as far as I can work out, except for the shoes, which are red. The clothes fit perfectly, clinging to me like a second skin. And the cloak spreads and lifts around me, almost like wings.

There's a rushing noise in my head as I finish. The world around me seems different somehow, more vivid, glowing. I can see all the little night creatures scurrying about in the undergrowth, and the trees wave and point as though trying to tell me something. The rushing noise is the noise of the river, calling to me with a thousand, thousand voices. Even the stones are murmuring to one another.

There's so much to see and hear that I can't take it all in. I look up and away from it all, towards Mabb's Hill.

What was it that Myrna said? *If you light a fire on Mabb's Hill, she will come to you.*

That's it then. That's where I have to go.

I take one step then another in my little pointy shoes. My footsteps are quick, darting along the river-bank. Seems like I only have to look towards where I'm going and I'm there. I'm speeding along the river towards the ford, then I have a sudden thought. I step out into the water, and instead of sinking, my foot slides over the surface. My cloak lifts, and I skim across the surface like a damselfly.

Takes me no time at all to get up that great hill. Time's turned into something else – I can almost hear it whizzing past my ears. I flit through the gorse and bracken, past all the stones that stipple the hillside, moving faster the higher I go, so that I can hardly think for speed, and for the voices of everything that's talking to me.

This is it, I'm thinking. *This is everything I've ever wanted!*

All the old Keri ever wanted was to be part of the magic of the world, and now I am!

Wildflowers open as I pass, calling to one another. *Stars like flowers in the sky*, they tell me. *Flowers like stars on the earth*. And in fact the stars do seem to be grouped together in some special way, in the same pattern as the flowers in the grass. And the flowers burn brightly, and the stars blaze back down at them.

Seems like everything's trying to talk to me, maybe it always was, and I never knew it before. *Many and one, many and one*, cries the grass, and the stones chant and rant and mumble with their stony tongues. And I want to listen, I do, but there are so many voices, and I can't stop. I carry on buzzing and flitting up the hill like a great, glowing insect.

And then at last I come to the summit. Stars blazing, trees waving, all the grass in motion, and through it all the river cuts a dazzling trail.

I knew the forest was big, of course, but I never knew, could never have imagined *how* big! It stretches on forever, just like Myrna always said, rolling and waving like a giant sea. The moon hangs above me, low and huge and brilliant, like I could just reach out and touch it. And it's so, so beautiful. I could stay up here and watch it forever.

But that's not what I'm here for. I'm here to find Mabb. And I don't know how.

I look around the stony hilltop. There's a bush

beside me, burning with life, and the stones are thrumming. But no Mabb.

I call her name. The wind takes my voice and carries it right round the world. It comes echoing back to me, 'MABB, MABB, Mabb,' but no one answers. I do it again, two or three times, just to hear the way it spreads out like ripples in water. The stones stir and the forest trembles, but there's no reply.

I have to light a fire.

Bryn once taught me how to light a fire, but I was never very good at it. You take a stick and rub it into a notch in another stick, for a long time, until smoke appears. The sticks have to be absolutely dry, that's one thing, and not green at all, that's another, and you have to have patience, that's the third, he told me, when I flung the sticks down and stamped off in a rage. I can still see him now, sitting with his legs stretched out, and the sticks between them, and a look of concentration on his face like he's calling to the fire to come. As though the fire was always there, inside the wood, waiting to be called.

When I look round now I can see that there is fire in everything, burning away in grass and stars and stone.

A thought takes shape in my brain and it goes something like this.

The old human me wasn't any good at making fire. Didn't have time for all that sitting around and rubbing sticks. But now I've changed. Don't feel human any more. Don't know what I am. I've been taken into the faerie world and come back different. That old Peggotty Witch called me Pixie.

Well, if I have changed and I'm not human any more, what am I? Part human, part faerie? And if I'm a faerie, maybe I can do magic.

The thought comes to me like a bright, glowing spark. I want to leap and shout, but instead I stand very still, looking around.

I can see the same fire in different things. Leaping and shimmering in shoots and blades of grass, dark and simmering in the heart of stones. But it's the same fire all right, everything, all around me is burning with it.

All I have to do is call it out.

I fall down to the ground and stare, eye level, at the grass. I can see it there, tiny sparks travelling from the root to the tip. My tongue flickers with the flickering of the spark. And suddenly I'm calling to it, calling to the fire to come out of the grass.

The flame flickers more brightly and I call to it some more. Don't know the words I'm using – my voice hisses and crackles and spits with the tongue of fire. The grass burns green before me and suddenly a spark shoots from the tip, smoulders and fizzles out. I dart back quickly, before I get singed, and stare, fascinated at the smouldering blade. Then I crouch down again.

Once again my tongue forms the words I don't

know, more confidently now. Sparks fizz from the blades, then fizzle out quickly as they meet the air. But then it happens. Two sparks meet one another, almost like kissing, and the grass ignites.

I carry on calling, calling in a hissing whisper, and everywhere small flames shoot from the blades of grass, leaping and dancing, and the smoke curls. Once the sparks meet there's no stopping them – fire travels quickly from one blade to another. Soon, it seems, the whole hilltop is ablaze.

Probably shouldn't have used the grass. There's no end to it. Small sparks start off greenish, then leap into yellow and orange. Smoke rises, and yellow and orange sparks whirl round in it, then fizzle out. But the fire's running now, all over the top of the hill. I stand still for a moment, fierce with pride, watching my handiwork. I'm not scared at all, though the fire's near my feet. The bush near to me bursts into flame and blazes merrily. Don't know how I'm going to stop it, but I don't even want to try.

The fire's beautiful – everything it touches curls and coils and shakes in a fiery dance. And soon I'm dancing too, leaping about and calling Mabb's name. If this doesn't summon her, nothing will.

'Mabb! Mabb! Mabb!' I shriek as the flames leap higher.

Don't know what I expect. Maybe that she'll step forward from the flames. She'll be angry that I've summoned her, and set fire to her hill, but I don't care. I go on dancing and leaping and shrieking until I'm entirely surrounded by flames. Feel like I'm part of the fire myself, and I never want it to end.

'Come out of your hole, Mabb!' I shriek. 'You can't hide from me! You took my life and I want it back!'

I go on like this, howling like a demon, but still she doesn't come. And the fire rages, burning everything it touches, but it doesn't touch me.

And it doesn't call up Mabb. Either she can't hear me or she won't come. I whirl round and round the hilltop, like one of the sparks in the smoke, but there's nothing, and no one.

I stop dancing and the fire starts to die down. I look all around in desperation. I can see shapes in the fire, but none of them looks like a faerie queen.

One of them looks like a doorway, though. An arched doorway, made of flame. At least I think I can see it, but the flames keep moving. Other shapes come and go, but the doorway's still there. And it's starting to open.

I look round again, at the dying fire, then back to the door. It's dying down too, though it's still opening. Any minute now it'll disappear, with the rest of the flames. Still I just stand there, panting and looking at the fiery door. My eyes are smarting from the smoke, and I rub them and look again, but it's still there. Just.

Only thing I can think is, I have to step into that door. Don't know where it leads to, or how I'll get back. Don't know that I won't just shrivel up and burn. I do know that if I don't do something, it'll just disappear, and I might not be able to call it back again. This might be my last chance of seeing that other world, of getting to Mabb. I don't know how I'm going to do that, but I've got to try, and I've got to try now.

And that's when I step into the fire.

PART III

I'm terrified, of course. Just for a second I feel its scorching heat, and I expect to burn to ashes any moment. But I've no time to think about it because the flames part in front of me, and there's a gust, like the blast of heat from a furnace, and I'm lifted right off my feet. The fire turns into a kind of tunnel, and I'm whisked along it, blown through on its fiery breath.

Faster and faster I whirl, like a spark in a tunnel of flame. There's no time to look around, but from the corners of my eyes I can see there are shapes in the fire, and the shapes are like trees, roots and branches. No time to wonder, or even think. The shapes are more solid now, and everything's darker. It's like looking at the roots of trees, down deep in the earth. Yet there's still a fiery glow.

Trees take shape all around me, and I tumble over and over, expecting to crash into one of them, but somehow I don't. And soon my feet are skimming over roots and fern and bracken on a forest floor. And it's just like the forest I remember, except everything's lit from within by this weird, fiery glow.

And it's *alive.* I always knew the forest was alive, but now I can hear it breathing, feel it looking at me. I can almost hear it think.

And I'm flying! Well, not exactly flying, but not walking either. My feet aren't on the ground. They're just brushing over it. I can feel a movement between my shoulders and I crane my neck round to look.

It's the cloak the Peggotty Witch gave me, greenish and shimmering. Thought before that it looked like wings, and now that it's spread out behind me, I can see that's exactly what it is. Wings. In beautiful, shimmering colours that catch all the light. And when I try to move them, I can. Some muscles I didn't even know I had quiver, and the wings quiver with them, and I start to move faster, flying through the forest of light.

All the time I'm thinking, *this is me, flying!* The old, ordinary me feels far away and long ago. This is the new me, and I'm magic!

My wings seem to know where I'm going, which is a good thing because I haven't a clue. And there aren't any paths. I'm flitting past trees, and over brambles. Small branches reach towards me as though wondering what I am, and blue-green ferns unfurl their feathery fronds. Soon as I start to think about where I'm going, I'm lost. Then the voices start.

'Over here, over here!'

'Not that way, this!' And so on. Takes me a moment to realize it's the forest itself that's talking, the deep, rasping voice of roots and stones, the high twittering voices of flowers and birds. I hover in mid-air while all the voices come together in a great jumble in my head, and the branch of a tree nearly grasps me.

Don't know which way to go any more. I change direction, dodging round a tree, and instantly the light changes, to a cold, greenish glow. There are faces in the moss on stones and the holes in the tree trunks are like gaping mouths. I flutter my wings backwards and the light changes to a warm glow. So now I know that something's guiding me, even if I don't know what.

No time to think. I flit and weave, letting my wings find the way. Flowers like jewels waggle their heads and chatter excitedly as I pass. Other winged, beautiful creatures brush past me and disappear. If I had time to think, I'd be stunned by the beauty of it.

Further on and the light changes again. Softer and more welcoming. Like the light of summer dreams, and friendship, or cherry blossom in May. Like falling asleep in your mother's arms or finding something you thought you'd lost forever. There's the sound of humming beyond all the chattering voices, a beautiful, sad tune, sweet and strange, yet familiar too.

I drift forward into that enchanted light, and feel

it cradling me. Beautiful memories flutter by on soft coloured wings and brush me with the lightest of feathery touches. Small acts of kindness whirl round like blossom in a breeze, and little rainbow-coloured hopes and dreams appear and disappear like bubbles on the surface of a pond. I fly among them in amazed delight that such a place could exist in the dark forest.

How could I not have known this before? I think. And *How could I ever want to leave?*

Seems like the tune's lulling me into sleep, but I'm resisting. Don't want to fall asleep before I find what I'm looking for. I came here to find Mabb, after all. So that's what I fix my mind on now.

I start to feel as though I know this place, or at least part of me does. It's the feeling that you can have in a dream, when you've always known that something is there. Trees and grass part in front of me, and here at last is a path, as I knew it would be.

The humming is sweeter and clearer as I follow it, and there's the sound of chattering and laughter. Yet somewhere in all the humming and laughter, there's the sound of weeping too. Then the path opens out into a clearing, like a chamber in the forest, and there it is.

A roundhouse. Just like one of the huts at home. Except that there's tangled ivy and honeysuckle all around it. And light pouring from it. I realize that all the light of the forest comes from here. And that this is where I want to be. I recognize it immediately. It's home.

Right in front of me there's a door. A small arched doorway, beautifully carved. With a little quiver of fear, I remember it. I know it's the door to Mabb's house, and that if I go in, I'll find her there.

There is the handle, shaped like a hand. I take hold of it, and it takes hold of me. The door glides open silently and the hand lets go, waving me in.

The sound of humming is louder now, and so is the weeping, a heartbreaking, lonely sound stronger than the humming, though still making a kind of music of its own. I brace myself against it, and look around.

I'm in Mabb's house all right. There's the little table that she called her *dressing table*, with something hanging over it, like a still pool. *Mirror*, she called it.

Now, of course, mirrors are something that the People just don't have. If you want to look at yourself, you look in water, in a pond, or a bowl. Yet I know exactly what this is, grey and glimmering against the wall, and it comes to me that I must know it from my time before, with *her*. I remember all the times I sat with her in front of that mirror, combing her beautiful hair. I remember trying to talk to her about going back home, just once, to visit the human world.

'What for?' she said. 'You would only feel sorry for them, with your soft, jelly heart. It is as soft as frog-spawn, your heart.'

'No, it isn't,' I said. 'I only want to laugh at them.'

But she wouldn't believe me, and the more I pleaded, the more suspicious she got. Her hair turned from shadows into thorns, and I had to start brushing it all over again.

Now, when I think of how she trapped me here and kept me prisoner, my heart burns fierce and cold, and I can't bear to look at the little table with its mirror any more. But everyhere else I look, there are things that remind me. A crystal basin full of tears for washing in, a chair of sighs. Then there are the shadows, flickering across the walls as if they're looking for something, or afraid they'll be found. One has its finger pressed to its lips, just like the reflection in the mirror. Others are running and hiding like they're playing hide and seek. I remember them. I used to try to talk to them on those long afternoons when Mabb would go out and leave me here, and I would get so bored, and lonely. But it was no use. They just carried on as if I wasn't there, trapped in their own shadow-play. A woman rocking a cradle, and an older woman spinning wool. And a man, like a hunter, who strode across the wall and disappeared into a mass of shadows. He was here before. I remember running after him because something about him reminded me of my father, but he ignored me, like all the others. Yet sometimes they seemed to know what I was doing. And now, as I pass, they all huddle together as though whispering. It's not a comfortable feeling, but I ignore them and land slowly on the floor. I walk, rather than fly, over to the windows.

There are four of them, one on each wall. When I look through the first one, it's winter, snow falling quietly, beautifully, in a wood. But in the next, it's spring, blossom whirling about or clinging to the branches with little wet, pink mouths. Summer in the third, with the rippling shadows of birds and clouds, and autumn, of course, in the fourth, wind whipping a thousand, thousand coloured leaves. And now my memory of this place is so powerful I can hardly remember anything else. I remember asking Mabb about the view from the windows, why it was winter in one and summer in another.

'All times exist here,' she said. 'And no time at all.'

And on another occasion she said, 'Shall we go out of the summer door?' And the window became like a door, swinging outwards, then we stepped outside and climbed into her chariot, which was like a hazelnut shell, and the creature pulling it had six legs and wings, and enormous eyes. There were round parts on either side of the chariot that made it roll in a way I had never seen before – round like spiders webs, or the heads of flowers, or the rays of the sun. I remember touching one of them in wonder before I got into the chariot, and asking Mabb what it was, but I don't remember what she said. Then she held her hand out to me and I climbed inside, and we skimmed through the grass that was as tall as trees.

Everything looked different then. Thread woven by insects clung to the grass like thick rope, droplets of water hung from them with whole shimmering worlds inside, and thistledown puffs flew overhead like clouds. We spent all that day cleaning the spines of baby hedgehogs, shaking the pollen from foxgloves or mending cracked eggshells with the silvery slime of snails. In every damp, sticky, oozing place we came to, giant insects extended their feelers into the soaking droplets that dripped from the fronds of ferns. And Mabb spoke to them in a strange language full of clicks and whirrs, and helped the baby caterpillars from their cocoons. Everything was more dappled, freckled and spotted than I ever knew, toads and leaves and fungus, snakes and reeds. Summer was almost autumn when we returned, exhausted, to our bed.

All these memories come flooding back to me now, as I gaze through the summer window, and then I notice the doors. Four of them. One door for each window.

I remember trying to make my own way through

those doors while Mabb was out, cautiously opening one, and leaping back in horror because suddenly I was on the edge of a cliff, so steep and sheer I could only see clouds far below. And when I opened the next one there was fire, and a third opened on to flood so that I had to slam it shut quickly, before the water lashed into the room. And when I opened the fourth, there was a storm so thick and hard and cruel, hailstones like little spears, that I wouldn't last a minute, I'd just be beaten down and lie buried in the snow. And I shut the door again quickly, trembling, and crept back into the bed.

That's when I remember the bed. Mabb's bed.

I turn round slowly, and there it is. Like a great shell. Gossamer curtains fluttering around it as though there's a breeze.

That bed – the bed I made. The curtains I spun, the coverlet of insect's wings! That's where the humming's coming from, of course. It's here now, in the centre of the room. The rest of my memories come flooding back as I look at it. I thought I'd be angry as a wasp, but as I look at that bed, all my anger seeps out of me. I can hear someone weeping in it, and my legs turn to water, and I can hardly move.

I glance back at the shadows. Sure enough, they've all turned to look at it. All the shadows on both sides of the room, facing that bed.

I take one step, then another towards it. It is the most terrifying thing I've ever done. With each footstep I can see the shadows tiptoeing with me. One of them, the little girl, still has its finger pressed to its mouth. It's separate from all the others, closest to me. When I look at it I remember why I've come here. My other memories, of this place, are so powerful that I've almost forgotten. But I've come here because I want to go home. I take hold of this thought and cradle it, like a candle flame in my heart.

The curtains part noiselessly, like clouds. Small tufts of cloud weave around the bed. I brush them away and they are soft and sticky on my hand. My head fills with the murmurings of insects on the coverlet, and the soft, musical weeping. I look down and there, like a pearl on the shell-shaped bed, is Mabb.

She is so beautiful, a beautiful little girl, just my own age, with her hair floating all around her pillow like moss in water. And she's weeping, softly, as though her heart will break. Everything I've ever been told about Mabb melts away as I look at her. She's not a terrible queen or a wicked enchantress. She's a girl like me, and she's weeping into her pillow.

The sound is so lonely and sorrowful that I just want to be with her. I bend over her as though to kiss her, and at the last moment she lifts up her face, which is wet with tears, and opens her eyes, which are the no-colour of rain, and as soon as she sees me, she lights up, like sun on water.

'Keri!' she says. 'Oh, you came back to me! I always knew you would!' And she opens her arms, and I fall into them, and I know at last that I'm back where I belong.

'Look at you,' she says, 'look at your funny clothes. What has happened to you?'

But I can't remember what's happened to me.

'You have suffered so much,' she murmurs, and her rainy eyes fill with tears once again. 'Was it so hard to come back to me? Was the journey so long and bitter?'

It was long and bitter – I remember that now. The longest and most bitter journey in the world. I'm overwhelmed with exhaustion, just thinking about it.

'You must rest and sleep,' she says, pressing me gently down into the bed. And the bed – the bed I made from cobwebs and thistledown and insects' wings and snail shells and cricket bones, that bed folds round me like a cloud. All I want to do is sleep, and dream the rest of my life away.

'You made the bed,' she says, 'and now you must lie on it.'

And that's what I do. I lie on it and sleep, cradled in her arms.

When I wake up I'm on my own again. The room is darker, and the curtains fluttering around me seem threatening somehow, blocking my view. I sit up and push them aside.

The room is there, just as I remember it. There is the chair of sighs, and the basin of tears. There is the little dressing table with its mirror, and all the windows, casting an eerie light into the room. The shadows seem to be standing to attention, like guards. One of them stands alone, though, the shadow of the little girl. I don't know why I think this, but it seems to be looking at me, and is definitely cross.

'What?' I say, looking back at it, but of course it doesn't answer. I get up then, and potter about the room. It follows me, pointing at things, but I ignore it. I splash my face with water from the basin of tears, then wipe it with my sleeve.

Where has Mabb got to? I remember how often she would leave me like this, and how much I hated it. I would wander round and round the room looking for something I couldn't remember, but when she came back, it was as though she had never left.

None of the shadows move as I go to look out of the autumn window. There is a quiet, still path in the woods, leaves drifting down, and a deer picking its way delicately across. The woods look so lovely, I wonder if she'll take me into them when she comes back, and how long she might be. When nothing happens, and she doesn't return, I try to open the window.

Instantly the wood changes, horribly. I can see that it's all made of bones. Small bones like twigs splinter and fall from skeletal trees to the ground, and the skeleton of a deer lies across the path. Then a tree opens its mossy mouth that is full of death, and a great voice cries, 'THIS IS THE REALM OF OLD BONES OF THE DEAD!'

I shut the window quickly and turn away, heart hammering. The room hasn't changed at all, and when I turn back to the window, there is the deer, and the quiet path, the leaves gently falling. But my stomach twists with fear and anger, because now I remember that I can never, ever, leave this room without Mabb.

I turn back again, slowly. There is the shadow of the little girl, on the opposite wall. She shakes her head vigorously as I look at her, then nods. She seems to be trying to tell me something. She stands very still as I cross the room towards her.

I go right up to her and trace the outline of her face and hair. Still she doesn't move, but when I put up my left hand towards her, her own hand raises and our palms meet.

Instantly my memories judder into life. Jumbled

and tumbling, pictures of my mother and Myrna, Digri and Bryn, then Lu as a baby, and the old man and woman I saw. And I remember, clear as a bell, Mabb's voice saying *you must leave me something in exchange.*

It's my shadow, of course. My shadow, that I had to leave here, with Mabb.

I stare, appalled and fascinated at my shadow on the wall, and my shadow stares back at me. I lift my other hand, and my shadow lifts hers. Then I lift my leg, and my shadow does the same. But when I step back from the wall, my shadow stays there, silent, watchful. I look all around myself on the jewelled floor. It's true. I have no shadow when I step back into the room.

I look back at my shadow on the wall, and she nods her head. It's really true, she seems to be telling me. I am your shadow. Mabb made you leave me behind when you went back to your world. That's how she knew you would return.

And that's how she changed me, so that when I went back to the human world, I wasn't human like them. Part of me remained here, with Mabb.

When I realize this, I feel a spark of pure rage. It surges through me until I want to leap and howl. Because I never left Mabb at all! She kept me here, all that time – even when I went back home my shadow was always here! She tricked me – and I don't know what to do about it. Because how can I get my shadow off that wall?

I go right up to my shadow once again. It waits, patiently, while I press my hand to its shadow hand, and move it away quickly, as though it might stick to the palm of my hand. But of course it doesn't. She lifts her hands with me, one at a time, then both together, and then she lifts her feet. It's as though she wants to, she's really trying, but she just can't leave that wall. I leap away from her in a rage and stamp my foot, but all she does is press her finger to her lips.

Then I stare at her in despair. 'What are we going to do?' I say.

For answer, she turns to one side. Still with her finger pressed to her lips, she starts tiptoeing across the wall. I follow her, and she leads me to the little dressing table. She stands to one side of it, pointing.

I look at the blank surface of the mirror. Can't even see myself in there. I remember now that I could only see myself when I was with Mabb. I don't like looking at it because it makes me remember all the times I sat with Mabb, brushing her hair. I remember the conversation we had about me going home, and how she told me I had a soft, jelly heart.

'I don't,' I told her. 'If it was that soft it wouldn't be breaking.'

And she said to me . . .

She said . . .

'Hearts don't break if you keep them in a casket.'

And that's when I look down, on to the table, and I see the casket.

It's a small silver casket, with a queerly shaped lock, like two hands clasping one another. I pick it up and look at it. Silver scrolls and swirls all over in a complicated pattern that looks like woven leaves if you hold it one way, and a spiral maze if you tilt it another. I shake it and it rattles, there's definitely something inside, and when I hold it to my ear I can hear it beating. Her heart!

I look at it in awe, then back at my shadow. She moves her hands as though opening it, but when I try to open the casket the little hands won't budge. I press it all over and shake it again – nothing. Probably like everything else in this place, it works by magic. I shake it once more and consider trying to smash it, but the metal looks hard and strong. I look at my shadow in despair. She only shrugs her shoulders.

Then a thought comes to me. *Hearts are opened by kindness.*

Don't know where that came from. I look quickly at my shadow, but she's standing very still. I look back at the casket.

I think of the poor heart, locked away in there, trapped and beating, trapped like everything else in this faerie place. How lonely it must be, without anything to love, how it has to go on beating, without hope of ever being set free. It seems like the saddest thought in the world. A tear forms in my eye, painfully like before, but this time I don't try to blink it back. I squeeze it out, and let it fall like a tiny tear-shaped jewel, towards the casket. And the little hands fly open and catch it, cupping it in their silver palms.

The lid lifts slowly on its own, and there, nestling in purple silk, is a tiny heart.

I've seen hearts before, when the pig gets slaughtered, or when Bryn and the others bring back a deer. They're all twisted and bloody with tangled veins. This heart isn't like that. It's heart-shaped, of course, but smooth and perfect, shimmering with soft, shiny colours. And somewhere inside it is a faint pulsing light.

It looks like stone washed smooth and shiny by water, but when I touch it, it feels warm, and it gives a little beneath my fingers. I realize that I could squeeze it, maybe even make it break. I slip it into the palm of my hand.

And then I hear the door opening on the far side of the room.

I've just got time to snap the little casket shut and return it to the table before I turn to face Mabb, trying to smile. My own heart's hammering and I can feel hers beating steadily between my fingers. She's looking at me curiously, but she isn't angry. 'Are you looking for something?' she says.

'No,' I say, moving a little way from the table.

She smiles then, and I can see she's carrying something on a large leaf. Flower cups and berries.

'I have bird milk here, and honey dew,' she says, carrying the leaf towards the bed. 'You must be hungry and thirsty after your long sleep. Won't you come and eat with me?'

She is all sweetness and goodness, her beautiful face turned up to mine. But as she moves towards the bed I feel rage like a splinter in my heart. I remember how I laboured to make that bed. It took not hours, not days or weeks, but years of my life, threading cobwebs together and sewing insects' wings. I made that bed at her bidding, and she took my life away. Anger twists my gut and I stay where I am, not following. She looks up at me, all puzzled innocence. Then she pats the bed.

'Come and eat,' she says. 'Afterwards we will sweep the forest floor.'

Rage bursts in me then, like when Myrna cut the abscess on my knee, yet somehow I keep it from boiling over.

'How long will that take?' I say lightly, though my heart is still hammering.

She looks at me as though she doesn't understand the question. 'There is no time here,' she says.

I'm advancing towards her now, fingering her heart. 'No – no time,' I say, stuttering with rage, 'not in your world – only in mine! You brought me here and you took my time away!'

Mabb's fingers touch her chest, where her heart should be. 'Keri,' she says reproachfully, 'I asked you if you wanted to stay with me and you did. Then I asked you to help me make this bed, and you did. When you asked to leave I sent you back.'

That stops me. I want to contradict her but I can't.

'Do you not remember asking me to come here?' she asks.

I do remember. I remember vividly asking her to take me, not Lu.

'Yes – but –' I say, struggling to put all my anger into words, to stop her from twisting everything, 'that was because my brother was ill – and I thought you'd taken him.'

She's still looking up at me, all innocence, with that luminous face.

'But that wasn't the only time you wanted to see me, was it, Keri?'

She's right. I know she is. I can feel the blood pumping in my ears. I can't explain to her why she's wrong.

'Did you take my father?' I blurt suddenly.

'Keri,' she says reproachfully. 'We've been through all this before. If I had taken your father, he would have been here, safe and well. I could not save your father, but I can save you. Do you not remember me telling you this?'

I do remember. I remember that every time she went out, I would look for Lu and my father. I would run round and round her house, looking for them, and was often in tears when she came back. Then she would comfort me, and make me forget.

'That is what it means to be human, Keri,' she says to me now. 'It means to lose everything you love. But here nothing is lost.'

I jerk my head towards the shadows then. 'What about them?' I say. Because now I realize that if my shadow's on her wall, then all those other shadows must belong to people too.

She doesn't answer me, but looks down at the coverlet, tracing a pattern of an insect wing with her finger.

'What have you done to them?' I ask her. 'Why don't you let them go? Why can't they go back to their own lives?'

She looks up finally, and there's a cunning expression in her eyes. 'What happened when you went back?' she asks.

But now my thoughts and words are jumbled so

that I can hardly speak. 'I-I went home –' I stutter.

'Yes?' she says, still looking up at me. 'Did they not welcome you?'

Pictures of my mother and baby Lu, then the old man and woman are scrambled together in my mind.

'They did not know me,' I say at last.

Mabb's head droops and she gives a melancholy sigh. 'Yes,' she says sadly. 'Human beings are like that. They remember nothing.'

She gets up then and begins to pace round the room. 'All the times I have tried to befriend them,' she says, 'all the times I have tried to tell them what I know. They turn their backs on me, Keri, they build their huts and walls and weave their feeble charms, and think that will keep me out. And from time to time a mortal encounters me, and I give them what they most deeply desire, and then . . .'

She lifts her hands up and there is an expression of grief on her face. 'Then they run away from me.'

She turns again and paces restlessly, then suddenly sinks back down on the bed. Her head droops sadly. 'They have made an evil witch of me, Keri.'

And even though I think, I *know*, that this isn't the full picture, I can't help seeing it through her eyes. How terrified people are of her, and of everything to do with faeries. How superstitious they are – how they make charms to ward them off, and tell stories against them, and build walls and huts and huddle inside them, desperate to keep them out. The faeries were here first, but we've driven them away.

'They are trying to make the land their own,' Mabb said. 'They do not want me, Keri. They do not want the magic.'

But I think suddenly of Bryn and Griff and the others, trying to build that dyke to stop the fields from flooding again, and how all their hard work planting seeds in the spring is useless in the face of one summer flood. And I think of Lu and Ogda, old and bent and alone, still struggling to survive, and I say, 'You could help them if you wanted to.'

'Oh, Keri,' Mabb says reproachfully. 'Do you not think I have tried?'

And then I think about Guri, bringing fire for the People, but how that cost him, and how he lost half his life. He had to leave his shadow with Mabb, just like me. Maybe his shadow is one of those on the wall.

'Well,' I say, struggling to get my thoughts clear, 'maybe they don't want to become shadows on your wall!'

Mabb's tongue flickers around her lips, then she holds out her hand towards me. 'You misjudge me, Keri,' she murmurs, tucking a strand of hair behind my ear. 'I never took anyone who didn't ask to come.'

'Don't!' I say, jerking away. 'You tricked me! You took my life away!'

'Your – life?' she says, and she gives a little laugh, like the tinkling of silver bells.

'Yes – my life!' I say, shouting now. 'I went back home. And everything – *everything* – had changed. Years and years had passed without me. No one was left – at least – two of them were. But – they didn't even know who I was!'

'You did not have to go back,' says that soft, soothing voice. 'You could have stayed with me.'

'No!' I shout. 'I did have to! I went home and my mother was – was . . .' But I can't bring myself to say the word 'dead'. I can feel those hard, painful tears in my eyes. 'She'd gone,' I say.

Mabb isn't looking at me. She's gone back to tracing the edge of a wing with her finger. 'And that's why you've come back to me now,' she says gently. 'Because there is no place for you there.'

'Yes – no!' I say, suddenly aware that she might be trying to trick me again. 'I want my old life back! Before you took all those years away from me! Before you robbed me of my time!'

She looks at me then, suddenly sly. 'How much time do you think has passed now?' she asks mildly.

I can hear a whooshing noise, like wind rushing

through my ears and all my blood runs cold. Because, believe it or not, I hadn't thought of that. Last time I was with her, forty years or more had passed. This time, hundreds and hundreds of years might have come and gone.

I make a small sound, midway between a choke and a whimper, and Mabb looks at me kindly. 'We can see if you want to,' she says. She crosses over to the dressing table and pats the stool. I look at her blankly. 'Let's look in the mirror,' she says.

Hope flares in my heart then, that she's going to show me something of my human life, the life I've lost. I might even see my mother, or my father. Still, I'm reluctant to sit with her at the dressing table, where I've spent so much time combing her hair. I cross the room slowly and perch on the edge of the stool, while she sits fully on it, and I can see her face clearly in its glimmering surface. This time I can see my reflection as well, but I don't like looking at it. It's pale and peaky, a little witchety face with huge, solemn eyes.

'Look,' says Mabb.

The surface of the mirror shivers and slowly clears. At first I can't see what it's showing me. Then slowly I realize that I'm looking at the huts and doorways of my settlement.

Everything is abandoned and deserted. The wind blows flurries of dust into the air. Rotting doors hang from the frames, and most of the roofs have fallen in. It looks old, older than it did when I last went back. There's a small movement to one side of the picture, and a little brown figure emerges, scurrying about. With a lurch of my stomach, I realize it's me. I'm scrambling around in all the debris, and though I can't hear myself, I know I'm calling out names. But no one comes, not even the little old man and little old woman that were Lu and Ogda. I'm all alone in the empty, crumbling village.

My stomach turns over, and I feel sick as I face my mother's hut. I walk in through the open doorway. I look all around. It seems deserted. Only a rat runs squeaking across the floor.

Then I hear a cough and see him, finally, lying crumpled on a mattress of straw.

'Ogda, Ogda,' Lu mumbles. 'You're taking a long time with that water.'

My heart twists with pity then. I know, somehow, that no Ogda will come. He's all alone.

I creep up to him.

He can't see me.

I look at him, then, greatly daring, put my hand out and turn his face. He doesn't seem startled by this, doesn't even seem to know what's happening.

He's much older, I can see that, and his eyes are worse. His hands shake all the time. And he carries on talking to Ogda, but Ogda isn't there.

I look round the empty shell of a hut. Doesn't look as though Ogda's been there for a while.

I can feel tears again, painful, pricking, but I blink them away. Daren't think about it now. There's work to be done.

'Don't be cross, Ogda,' he says.

There's no food to be found in the hut. I go outside and look for the hens. No hens, no pig. I go back into the hut. Pick up the broom and sweep it. Then I collect the remaining wood from the wood pile and light a fire. He turns his face towards it, his blank eyes open. 'You're back then,' he says.

'I am,' I say. 'I won't leave you again.'

I touch his hand and he catches hold of it and presses it to his cheek.

'Ogda,' he says.

'Oh, Lu,' I say, 'sweet baby brother – I'm here, I've come back, I won't ever leave.'

My words are like the murmuring of the wind, but he grunts a little as though pleased, and closes his eyes.

I talk to him then, about our mother, and Myrna and Digri and Ogda, the way she used to be, and how we all played in the forest in the old, old days that seem as long ago as the dawn of time. And soon his breathing changes, and I can tell he's asleep.

But I sit with him, and my heart is breaking. I will stay with him, of course, until the end of his days. I will help him, though he can neither see nor hear me. We will be company for one another. But then what?

Don't know if I can die.

Don't even know if I can sleep.

I wish, with all my heart, that I hadn't come back here.

My breath catches, ragged in my chest. 'That's not what I meant!' I cry, turning to Mabb. 'That's not what I want to see!'

'No?' she says, and she waves a hand at the mirror.

The picture mists over, and once again starts to clear. This time I see trees. Trees shifting and blowing about. The picture won't stop moving and I realize that I'm seeing it as though moving through the forest. One hut, then another appears, then my heart beats thick and strong as I see people, my People, coming from the huts. Bryn, holding a lantern, and Griff and Digri behind him, then Arval and Gwern, and Mabda, holding a lantern of her own. Then at last I see my mother, her auburn hair flying as she hurries up the hill towards the forest. I move towards the mirror with a cry.

'Don't touch it,' Mabb says, sudden and sharp. Then, more softly, 'It's only a picture, remember.'

But it seems so real. I make a small sound of pain as they lift their faces towards me, and I realize slowly, painfully, that they can't see me at all.

But they're looking at something – something coming out of the forest. My gaze turns with them, and my heart shifts as I stare at a little, ragged, white-faced urchin, stumbling from the trees into my mother's arms. And she's so relieved to see me she can't even speak, not even to tell me off. She hugs me and strokes my hair, and we turn and hurry back towards the huts.

But then the images move faster. I'm living with the People again – my People, but it's as though I've become a stranger. Looking with hollow eyes at my mother and Bryn, who will get old and die, and Digri who will die in a fall, and Lu and Little Ogda, who will grow old together, but alone. I move among them in a dark dream, haunted by what I know, and getting no older myself. And sometimes the knowledge slips out of me, and the people I love best look at me as though I'm some uncanny thing, and make the sign of the evil eye. And when I grow no older they whisper about me in secret, and when my mother dies, they drive me away . . .

'Stop it! Stop it! Stop it!' I shriek, and I bound up from the bed and away from the terrible images in the mirror. I curl up tight in a corner of the room, burying my face in my knees so I can't see anything. A great sob tears its way out of my chest.

Though I'm not looking, I can feel Mabb standing over me, but I shrug her away violently when she tries to touch me.

'Poor Keri,' she says, 'poor, poor Keri.'

I look up then. 'You did this,' I say, pointing at her. 'You! You've taken everything away from me!'

I can hardly speak, I'm so angry, and I don't want to burst into tears in front of her. She'd like that – the old witch.

But she isn't angry. Her face is full of gentle mourning. 'Keri,' she says, 'don't you see I gave you everything you ever wished for?'

I shake my head. I can't even speak any more. I'm so angry, all the words are jammed up in my throat.

'You wished for a playmate, and I gave you one. You wanted to be like me, and I helped you. Then you wanted to return. I was sad, of course I was, but I let you go. Only I didn't want to send you back old and feeble, so I gave you your youth. I gave you back the years you'd lost.'

I stare at her. Everything she says is true. At least, she can't see she's done anything wrong. She really can't. She's looking at me, all hurt innocence, and I can't help but see it through her eyes. She has given me everything.

'But now I've got nothing,' I say, 'and no one.'

The look on her face. Shocked, hurt, reproachful. 'You have me,' she says. 'You can stay here.' But I only groan and bury my face in my hands.

Then she crouches in front of me. 'Stay with me,'

she murmurs. 'You have a life here, with me. People come and go, they forget things, they change their minds and their hearts, time wastes them away and they grow old and die. But here you will never grow old.'

She leans forward and grasps my closed fists. 'Stay with me, Keri,' she urges. 'You have lost everything, you have no one – I have no one too. All my people have fled. We could be everything to one another. Don't you understand what I'm offering you? You could leave behind your mortal life and live with me forever!'

And in a flash then, I see how it could be – me and Mabb playing in our enchanted forest, stringing spiders' webs from branches, drinking nectar from flowers, teaching the baby birds to fly. No more sickness and pain, no more loneliness, no more growing old and dying. We would live forever, learning the language of stones and trees, and all the brightness and magic and fire of the faerie world would be ours.

'You cannot want to return to your mortal world,' she says, 'to old age and sickness and death. Those people you call yours do not even know you, Keri, they don't know how much you have to give. They will forget you, Keri. So much time has passed that they have already forgotten you. But I have nothing to do with time,' she says, still holding on to me.

'Years come and go. What have they to do with me?'

I pull back from her, wrenching my fists away. 'But they've got everything to do with me!' I tell her. 'I'm human, and I need to be with humans. I want my home back and my family, and I want them back now!'

She looks at me with a peculiar expression on her face, a queer, half-smile of triumph. 'You *were* human,' she says gently, and all my breath catches in my throat. Then it's my turn to grab her by the arm.

'Listen to me, you evil witch,' I hiss. 'I don't know what you've done to me, but you can undo it. I want my old life back – just the way it was before I met you. I wish I never had met you. So spin your webs and cast your magic spells, and send me back now!'

She rises then and stands up, tall – taller than she has ever been. Not a little girl any longer, but the Faerie Queen, tall as a young tree, older than time.

'You do not tell me what to do,' she says. Her voice is like lightning, flashing inside my skull, and her heart beats rapidly in my hand. I stand up too, and hold it up so that she can see it.

'What's this then?' I say.

For the first time I see an expression like fear flit across her face. She lifts her hand to where her heart should be, in her chest. For a moment neither of us says anything, then her head droops.

'Oh,' she says. 'You have come to kill me.'

'I will kill you,' I say, 'if you don't send me back. Back to the way things were before.'

Her heart is soft and palpitating between my fingers. I could crush it so easily. I can hear my own heart beating fast and strong. I squeeze her heart, and she clutches her chest with a moan and starts to sink to the floor. But she looks up at me, and her tender, rain-coloured eyes are full of tears.

'Kill me then, if you must,' she says.

Crush it, crush it, a voice says in my head. Yet still I hesitate. For one thing I can see, suddenly, clearly, that if I kill her, I have no idea what will happen next – which world I'll go back to, or even if I can get back at all.

And I can see also that if I kill her, all the enchantment and magic of this world will fade – all its mystery and cruelty. She does what she does for no reason at all – just because it's in her nature – because she can. And what she does is beautiful in its own way. Simply, eerily, beautiful.

I can't kill her, I see that now. I can't kill her just for being herself. Whatever is left of me that's still human can't do it.

That's when I know I'm not all faerie, whatever she says. Part of me is human, and that part can't save me now.

I release the pressure on her heart and let my hand fall uselessly by my side.

'I don't want to kill you,' I say. 'I just want to go home.'

She doesn't look at me. She is crouching, still holding her chest where I hurt her.

'But what if I can't send you home?' she says.

There it is. The words I've most dreaded to hear. She might be able to change things, but can she change them back?

'You must be able to,' I say, and she gives a slight, very small, shake of her head.

Don't know if I believe her or not. I do know, now, that I can't make her do anything she doesn't want to do. My legs start to tremble and my stomach feels sick. I make my way over to her bed, almost stumbling, and sink down on it. All I can see in my mind are the images she showed me in the mirror, of Lu grown old and dying, then me growing old and mad and a stranger in my own world. I shake my head but I can't shake them out of it. Seems like I've got two choices, only neither of them's what I want. But I can't stay here. That's not even a choice any more. I shake my head again, as if I can make it clearer. Then I say, 'I'll go back anyway.'

She looks at me incredulously. I can see that she's shaken. 'Go back – to *that*?'

I nod once, heavily. I will go back, no matter what. To whichever world is waiting for me.

'You *want* to grow old?'

I don't say anything.

'And watch everyone you love grow old – and die?'

I still say nothing. But I can see from her face that she doesn't believe me, that she simply doesn't understand. And I don't know why, but I have to try to make her understand. Maybe it's just that I have to understand it myself.

'At least I'll be able to love them,' I say, and I realize, even as I'm saying it, that it's true. You need the time in things to be able to love. You need the change in them, you even need the death. Because that's what makes them precious.

'You don't love anything,' I say, and I realize that's true as well. Whatever she wants, she takes. And changes it into something else.

Mabb's face flickers for a moment, but she doesn't speak. I speak to her instead. 'You want me to stay with you,' I say, 'as your plaything – for your amusement. You call that love – but it isn't love – you don't know how to love – it isn't anything – it's nothing at all.'

Mabb is glimmering white and shaken by my words.

I can see the anger in her, but more than that, for the first time, I see how thin and white and spidery she looks. But still she's determined to pretend that nothing's wrong.

'Keri,' she says, 'if you stay with me, you will forget . . .'

I look at her then, and into that look I put everything I've lost, everything she's taken from me, and how the last thing in the world that I would want to do is to forget, but all I say is, 'You've made me lonely.'

It doesn't seem enough, anywhere near enough, after everything I've been through, and everything I'm going through right now, but the funny thing is, it seems to hit home.

Her face changes. An expression like horror flits across it. I can see, in that moment, what I've never seen before in all the time of knowing her. All the time I've been with her, she's made me see the world through her eyes, but now I've made her see it through mine. And she doesn't like it at all. I can see her struggling with it, as though she's had a thought she's never been capable of thinking before. She presses her fingers to her forehead. Her lips are working as she tries to see herself in her world, but no sound comes, and the moment seems to go on forever. She seems even thinner and shinier, more spidery. I turn away from her.

'I'm going back now,' I tell her.

'Stop!' she says in a strangled voice, and I do stop, but I don't turn round.

'Aren't you going to ask me which world you can go back to?' she says in a thin, spindly, wheedling voice. 'Aren't you even going to ask me for three wishes?'

I hesitate then. Three wishes. What could I not wish for? That I had my old life back? That Lu would be well again? And even, that my father had not died. I could wish that no one I loved would ever die. My thoughts race, and my heart races with them. But then I remember, suddenly, clearly, that that's how I got into this mess in the first place. Wishing for a life I didn't have. Wishing for things to be different from what they were. Wishing that I could enter the faerie world. And all my wishes came true, and it's just like a nightmare. I've lost everything I ever loved. I've wished myself lonely.

If I had more wishes now, wouldn't that make me just like Mabb? Cruel and cold, wanting everything my own way, changing everything to suit me? And wouldn't part of me always belong to her?

So I turn, finally, and her heart in my fingers gives a single great throb. I walk over to her and she has a hungry, fierce expression on her face.

'You can keep your three wishes, Mabb,' I say, and I lift up her heart, then press it into her chest. She gives a little gasp and a shudder as it enters into her.

'You choose,' I tell her, and I walk away.

Then behind me I hear Mabb's cry. High and shrill and lonely it sounds, then higher, and shriller. The walls of her room rock and judder, the doorway splits in two as I reach it. I leap through it, and there's another room like the one I've just left, only dusty, and old and dim. There's the chair of sighs and the basin of tears, and the little dressing table with its mirror. There's a crumbling noise, and the ceiling starts to fall in. I dash through the splitting doorway just in time.

And I'm in the same room once more. The chair of sighs is broken and the basin of tears cracked and mouldy. Everything's strung with cobwebs or crumbling into ash. Desperately, I run towards the door again. I turn the handle.

I'm in the same room again but it's crumbling all around me. Small stones shower down on me and cracks appear beneath my feet. Don't seem to have wings any more, I'm not flying, just stumbling on, – a small scared figure pursued by flying stones. I'm clinging to one wall and going as fast as I can because now all the walls are shaking with Mabb's cry. And still the cry gets higher, louder and more unbearable. It has all the agony and sadness in the world.

Faster and faster I go as the floor trembles and

threatens to shake me off my feet. No matter how fast I go, I hardly seem to be moving.

I'll never make it, I think. *I'll be buried here in a pile of rubble between the worlds, and Mabb and all that goes with her will be buried with me.*

It's then that I see my shadow, running frantically ahead of me, along the wall. I'm skidding on sharp rock and thrown from side to side by great quakes, and there's a sudden grinding, rumbling noise as the roof itself begins to split. I try to catch up with my shadow, but she's always a little way ahead.

The distance between us is widening. Soon we'll be separated forever. She's waving at me wildly, and then I see it. The mirror above the dressing table, on the far wall.

The table's just a heap of broken wood, but the mirror's still there, hovering like a still pool in the air. It's not gleaming any more, it's a blank darkness and I can't see anything in it. But my shadow's standing next to it, waving frantically.

The room is collapsing behind me as I run. And I'm running for all I'm worth, but still it seems to me that I'll never reach that mirror. I'll be buried in rocks, and nothing will matter any more. The floor splits, and I leap right across it. Then the mirror starts to crack.

On the wall next to me, my shadow makes a jumping motion, and disappears then reappears again.

She wants me to jump into the mirror.

I shake my head vigorously.

'I can't!' I cry, but my words are lost in all the rumbling, crashing noises. It's no use. I can't leap into that glassy surface. Don't know where I'll land. A shower of small stones strikes my shoulders, but still I don't move. No way forwards, no way back. I stare hopelessly at my shadow, and my shadow stares at me. Then slowly, as if saying goodbye, she holds up her hand.

Even though I know there's no point, I hold my hand out to touch her for the last time.

And that's when I feel her shadowy fingers holding mine, like feathers in my palm. I close my fingers round them, and she steps away from the wall. The ground beneath us falls away to an immense abyss, all livid lights and jagged edges. Behind us, the chamber collapses in an avalanche of rubble. The mirror splits slowly, opening on to more darkness. Don't suppose I'll see anyone I love ever again. But at least I'm not alone now. The two of us, girl and shadow, leap into the dark surface of the mirror.

All the air whooshes out of me. I'm plummeting so fast I can't think. Just as well, when you're about to be dashed to bits. All I can think is, *this is it, now*, as the darkness rushes up to meet me.

Then I see it, a kind of wrinkle in the darkness. No

time to wonder what it is; no time to shout. I hang on to my shadow and together we plunge into it. Feels like the world's folding up around me.

And that's it. I leap into the air, over a valley of stones, but I land on my back in the forest, legs and arms flung wide, both eyes open, staring.

Everything around me is in motion. It's dark, but there's a pattern of branches above me. Trees, shifting and blowing about. I can hear the rustle of grass in my ears. There's breath in my body, and I know I'm alive.

Cautiously, I move one foot, then the fingers of one hand, then the other. Nothing broken. Slowly, I sit up. The forest murmurs and stirs all around me. Can't see my shadow, it's too dark. I try to work out where I am. Leaves have fallen and I'm lying on a thick bed of them. My ears are filled with strange noises, rustling and creaking and moaning, like the forest is alive. Well, I knew that, of course. I get up on my knees, then slowly, unsteadily, stand.

Heavy. Everything seems heavy. My arms and legs feel like they're made out of stone. Except they're bruised, and aching. Didn't know a body could be this heavy.

Maybe it's my heart, weighing it down. Because I know I'm back, but I don't know what I'll find. My stomach is hollow with fear. I take one stumbling step, then another. This is what it feels like, to be mortal.

Trees, and more trees, shifting and blowing about.

Don't know if I'm going in the right direction, because all I can see is trees.

Then I see something else. A light, flickering in the branches like a fallen star. I move towards it, as fast as my heavy body will let me. I try to call out, but my tongue feels like it's made out of wood, and all my breath catches in my side. The trees start to clear, and I glimpse the roof of one hut, then another. Then someone calls out my name.

My heart beats thick and strong as I see them – Bryn and Griff and Gwern, carrying lanterns up the hill. They look up and Bryn calls out again, and I realize that it's me they're looking at, they can see me! A little ragged urchin coming from the trees as fast as she can. Bryn and Gwern move apart and I can see her, finally – my mother, coming up the hill with her face all puckered up with worry.

Now I'm running and tumbling so fast I can't stop. My mother's face changes to startled hope. 'Keri!' she cries, and suddenly everyone's shouting, calling to one another, but I can't even hear. I stumble into my mother's arms and bury my face in her, and she's warm, so warm, and I can smell her, the smell of cooking and herbs and sweat, and I can hear her real, her human, heart.

And that's it. That's how I go back to my ordinary life. Shelling peas, weaving baskets, scaling fish. And looking after my little brother, Lu.

Lu's all right.

When I looked up finally from my mother's arms, the first thing I said was 'Lu?'

'Lu's fine,' she said. 'He's sleeping in his cradle.' And I felt such a rush of relief I could hardly walk. I stumbled back with her to the hut. And there he was, my little brother, his face round and rosy again, with no trace of the rash. My eyes filled with tears, real human tears, and I brushed them away. Then I touched the amulet round his neck.

'Don't wake him,' my mother said quickly. 'He's been in a terrible mood all day, with his teething.'

'But – he was ill,' I said, and my mother looked at me strangely.

'He had a bit of a fever,' she said, 'but it was only his teeth coming.'

I stared at her then. 'But he was really ill,' I wanted to say. Only it was as though I could no longer remember what had happened and what hadn't. I struggled to get my thoughts together, but all I could do was yawn.

'Time for bed,' my mother said briskly. 'You can tell us all about it in the morning.' And she led me through to my bed, my own lovely bed, which was just the way I remembered it, and I lay down on it and she tucked me up. And she kissed me, which was something she hardly ever did.

'I'm so glad you're back,' she said, in a trembling voice. And she stayed with me, stroking my hair, until I fell asleep.

In the morning I wake up from the deepest sleep I've ever known, in my own bed, in my own hut, and the first thing I do is run into the main room to check that they're all still there. My mother's stirring the porridge and Lu is sitting on the floor, splashing his hands in his bowl. I run to him and gather him up, and he squawks and pushes me away. Then he pats porridge on to my face and my mother laughs.

'Don't worry about him,' she says. 'That tooth's still bothering him.'

And that's it. No mention of him being near death. No mention of me running away into the forest. No one asks me what I did there. It's as though they're all just glad to have me back home. So I don't mention it either. And I don't ask how long I was gone. I'm here now.

Myrna comes with a herbal brew she's made, and looks at me keenly as I drink it.

'Where've you been?' she says. 'Away with the faeries?' and I look at her sharply, wondering how much she knows. She smiles, and looks away from me, and suddenly I know, I should've known all along. *Myrna's been there too.*

That little girl they found, separate from all her clan, with the strange gifts and stories, who's lived so much longer than the rest of us. She'd been with the faeries just like me. I open my mouth to ask her, but she just touches my cheek. 'No talking just yet,' she says gently.

Weird thing is, I can't speak. Whenever I try to tell my mother what happened to me, something happens in my head, and my memories shift so the words come out different and I'm talking about something else. Eventually I stop trying. I hardly speak at all that first day, but watch what's going on around me, as though I've never seen it before, as though I'm afraid that I'll forget it all – Bryn mending the thatch on the roof, the fire sputtering and crackling. *I've chosen this world,* I think. This ordinary, beautiful world.

Then Digri comes to visit, with little Ogda. Seems strange, seeing her now, after seeing her as an old woman. I don't feel like playing. I don't want to leave my mother and Lu, but she gives me a little push.

'Go on and play,' she says. So for the first time I step out of my hut.

I see my shadow in the autumn sun, long and spindly, with Digri's shadow, and Ogda's.

'My shadow!' I say, and they look at me like I've gone daft. I lift my hand, and my shadow lifts hers. But it's only a shadow. It can't talk back to me and it doesn't want to play. I look all around me then, and none of it seems real. It feels as though I'm dreaming, and I'll wake up soon, and none of it'll be there. I stand still, staring at all the familiar sights.

There's a kind of smoke about early winter, mist rising from the river, curling up from the earth itself, and down from the clouds lowered over the fields. Smoke curls upwards from hearths and wreathes into it and even the sun is misty, shining through a smoky haze. I can hear the men working on the dyke, trying to finish it before the winter sets in, and Mabda smiles at us, carrying a basket of apples on her hip. I feel a terrible fear then, that it will all disappear soon, and I will be alone again, in Mabb's world.

'Are you coming to play or what?' Digri says, and I follow him down to the river.

Gradually, as I play with the others, with Digri and Peglan and Arun and Ogda, the memory of Mabb's world fades, as though that was the dream, terrible, and lonely and enchanting.

At the same time, and I can't describe it any other way, I'm struck by a powerful sense of loss. The crying of a bird pierces through me, and I look up at the light in the far distance, where sky and earth are blue. Then I look at the others, who are absorbed in their playing, just to remind myself that this is real.

Finally, I look up at Mabb's Hill.

The light changes around us. Everything turns brown and grey. A few drops of rain fall, making circles in the brown water. The stones are wet and dark, the fungus on them a luminous green. Darkness seeps up from the earth and mist floats down from the sky. I can hear the river rushing on, but I can't hear what it's saying any more. The trees are heavy and dark and silent. All the colour and light is draining out of the world.

Digri looks up. 'We'd best get back,' he says, picking Ogda up.

I can't help feeling cheated as I follow them slowly back to the huts. Back to all the jobs I have to do. Back to the hut where my mother lives with Bryn, where my father no longer lives. I fall behind the others, thinking about everything I've lost. Thinking that I wish I'd brought something back with me, like Guri. Something that proved it had all really happened. I even wish I could see the Peggotty Witch one more time. I wouldn't chase her again, or try to drive her away with sticks and stones.

The rain comes down harder, and brown pools form in the grass. I look down into one, and see my reflection – the real, ordinary me.

Then just as I'm straightening up, I see something else. Another reflection. The reflection of an old grey woman, wrapped in a shawl. *The Peggotty Witch!* I think. But even as I stare down at it, it lifts its face, and it's Mabb's face. I'm staring down at Mabb!

I bend so far down over the water I nearly fall in.

And she looks at me as though she's trying to speak, as though she's sorry. Then she blows me a kiss.

The kiss rises like a bubble to the surface, and I reach out and touch it with my finger. The bubble stays on my finger, and as I lift it up, its shining surface changes.

I straighten up slowly, staring at the shining object that's growing now, in the palm of my hand. It's a little chariot, just like the one I travelled in with Mabb, that was made from an empty hazlenut shell, with the round parts on either side that make it roll. They are like, but not like, the logs the men use to roll stones to the river. I touch it with my finger and make the round parts move, and I remember how I touched one of the rounded ends before.

'What is it?' I asked her, and her voice comes back to me now, just as if I'd never left her.

'It's a wheel, Keri,' she says. 'Nothing magical. It's just a wheel.'

'Wheel,' I repeat now, moving the round parts with my finger. 'Wheel.'

There's a stick underneath the chariot that connects the moving parts. It's like the rollers that the big stones move on, only thinner, because the rollers are just smooth logs. If they were hewed away so that they were thin in the middle and round at both ends, like the parts of this chariot, they would roll much more easily.

I'm standing in a pool of water in a muddy field, and it comes to me like a flash of pure magic, how much difference that would make – how this one little *wheel* could change all our lives.

What was it Griff said – *we need another Gift.* I touch it again and I know this is it – another Gift all the way from Faerie – from Mabb, Queen of the Faeries, to me, Keri.

Keri's Gift.

The Whispering Roads

Wherever you go, the past will follow . . .

'Vivid and powerful' – Funday Times

'A powerful and quite extraordinary novel'
– Berlie Doherty

Annie is strange – she has visions, hears voices in her head.

Her brother, Joe, just longs for freedom.

They're on the run. The question is, where? Because it's hard to feed yourself on whispers and lies, and the road ahead is a long and dangerous one . . .

puffin.co.uk

It all started with a Scarecrow

Puffin is well over sixty years old.
Sounds ancient, doesn't it? But Puffin has never been
so lively. We're always on the lookout for the next big
idea, which is how it began all those years ago.

Penguin Books was a big idea from the mind of
a man called Allen Lane, who in 1935 invented
the quality paperback and changed the world.
**And from great Penguins, great Puffins grew,
changing the face of children's books forever.**

The first four Puffin Picture Books were hatched in 1940 and the
first Puffin story book featured a man with broomstick arms called
Worzel Gummidge. In 1967 Kaye Webb, Puffin Editor, started the
Puffin Club, promising to **'make children into readers'.**
She kept that promise and over 200,000 children became
devoted Puffineers through their quarterly installments of
Puffin Post, which is now back for a new generation.

Many years from now, we hope you'll look back and
remember Puffin with a smile. **No matter what your age
or what you're into, there's a Puffin for everyone.**
The possibilities are endless, but one thing is for sure:
whether it's a picture book or a paperback, a sticker book
or a hardback, **if it's got that little Puffin
on it – it's bound to be good.**